The Skeleton's Lens

By Jo Smoak

Second Edition

Dedication

To the memory of those lost, and the strength of those who never gave up.

Preface

The world is full of shadows. Secrets lurk in the corners of our minds, hidden in the dust of forgotten memories. Sometimes, the most chilling truths are those that remain unspoken, the wounds that never heal. "The Skeleton's Lens" delves into one such truth, a story whispered in the silence of a long-lost sister's disappearance, a chilling tale of family secrets, and a detective haunted by the past.

As you turn these pages, prepare to journey into the darkest recesses of human nature, where the lines between truth and deception blur, and the shadows of the past stretch out to touch the present. This story is not for the faint of heart, but for those who dare to seek the truth, even when it threatens to consume them.

Introduction

The click of a camera shutter, a single, blurry photograph, and the echo of a name lost to time. These are the threads that weave the tapestry of "The Skeleton's Lens," a story that unfurls like a forgotten film reel, revealing a glimpse into the heart of a chilling mystery.

Detective John Snider, a man haunted by the unsolved disappearance of his sister, Sarah, is thrust back into the past when a skeleton holding a vintage camera is discovered. The camera holds a single, blurry photograph – a fragment of Sarah's final moments, a chilling testament to the enduring power of a single image. The photograph, a ghostly whisper from the past, becomes John's lifeline to the truth, propelling him into a desperate race against time.

As John pieces together fragments of the past, he discovers a web of family secrets, long-buried resentments, and a killer who has been lurking in the shadows for decades. His journey is a relentless pursuit of justice, a quest to confront the chilling reality that his sister's killer has been living among them all this time.

But what begins as a personal quest for answers soon evolves into a harrowing investigation that threatens to shatter everything John holds dear. The search for the truth, like the camera's lens, unveils a dark side to humanity, exposing a hidden world of deception, betrayal, and the chilling consequences of unresolved grief.

"The Skeleton's Lens" is a gripping mystery that weaves suspense, family drama, and the enduring power of love with the chilling reality of a long-lost sister's tragic fate. It is a story that will stay with you long after the last page is turned, a chilling testament to the secrets that linger in the shadows of our past.

Chapter 1: The Shadow of the Past

The air hung heavy in the detective's office, thick with the dust of time and the weight of unspoken memories. John Snider, a man etched with the lines of years and the furrows of unsolved cases, stared at the grainy photograph in his hand. The image, captured by a vintage camera found clutching the skeletal remains of an unknown woman, held a faint glimmer of hope, a fragile thread in the tapestry of his sister's disappearance.

Sarah, his younger sister, had vanished twenty-five years ago. The years had peeled away, leaving behind a gaping hole in the fabric of John's life. Her absence, a constant ache in his chest, had become a relentless companion, reminding him of the unfulfilled promise of their childhood, their laughter echoing in the now silent hallways of their shared memory.

The discovery of the skeleton, unearthed during the construction of a new shopping mall, had rekindled a spark of hope in John's weary heart. The camera, a relic of a bygone era, held the potential to unlock the secrets of the past, to reveal the truth that had eluded him for so long.

As John scrutinized the photograph, he felt a surge of adrenaline course through his veins. The image, though blurred, offered a fleeting glimpse of a shadowed figure lurking behind Sarah, a figure John believed he recognized. The photograph was a ghost of Sarah's final moments, a silent testament to the terror she had endured. It was a puzzle piece, a fragment of a horrifying truth that John was desperate to assemble.

He had spent years chasing shadows, seeking answers in the whispers of the past. Every dead end, every false lead, had been a nail hammered into the coffin of his hope. The photograph, however, was different. It was tangible, a physical embodiment of his sister's last moments, offering him a concrete starting point in his relentless pursuit of justice.

John's mind raced, replaying the memories of Sarah's disappearance. The last time he had seen her, she had been leaving their family home for a night out with friends. He remembered her infectious laughter, the twinkle in her eyes, and the way her hair had framed her face like a halo of golden sunlight. He had waved goodbye, little knowing that it would be the last time he would see her alive.

The following day, a wave of terror had washed over their family. Sarah was gone, her whereabouts unknown. The police had conducted a thorough investigation, but their efforts had yielded no answers, leaving the family stranded in a sea of unanswered questions.

The weight of his sister's unsolved case had become a heavy burden on John's shoulders. It was a burden he had carried for years, a constant reminder of his inability to protect his sister from the horrors that had befallen her. The photograph, however, had reignited a flame of hope, a fierce determination to find answers, to avenge the pain and terror his sister had endured.

John knew that the photograph held the key to unlocking the truth. He knew that it was his responsibility to decipher its cryptic message, to bring his sister's killer to justice. He was determined to follow every lead, to pursue every whisper of the past, until he found the answers he desperately sought.

He knew that the road ahead would be fraught with danger, that the shadows of the past could be treacherous, but he was not deterred. His determination was fueled by the memory of his sister, her laughter, her love, her life that had been stolen from her. He would find her killer, no matter the cost. He would bring him to justice, for Sarah, for his family, and for the peace that had eluded him for far too long.

The photograph lay on his desk, a silent sentinel of his sister's final moments, a guide in his quest for truth. It was a promise, a commitment to Sarah, to find the answers that had eluded him for so many years. He would find the truth, even if it meant confronting the darkest corners of the past, even if it meant facing the demons that had haunted him for years. He would find Sarah's killer, and he would never stop until he brought him to justice.

John held the photograph, its edges worn and faded, a testament to the passage of time. The image itself was blurry, almost ghostly, a snapshot captured in a fleeting moment. Yet, within its grainy depths, John saw a glimmer of hope, a possible path to unravel the mystery that had haunted him for decades. The photograph, taken with a vintage camera found clutched in the skeletal hand of the unearthed remains, was the only tangible clue to Sarah's fate.

He scrutinized the image, his gaze drawn to the figure standing in the shadows behind Sarah. It was a hazy silhouette, almost indistinguishable, but John felt a shiver run down his spine. The figure, a man shrouded in a darkness that seemed to seep from the edges of the photograph, seemed familiar. John traced the lines of the figure's outline, his mind racing, trying to connect the shadowy image to a face, a name, a memory.

The camera had captured a fleeting moment in time, a glimpse into Sarah's final moments. John wondered if the figure was a witness, a passerby, or something more sinister. The possibility that the figure was the one who had taken Sarah from him, who had extinguished her light, sent a jolt of fear through him.

The blurry image, with its haunting silhouette, felt like a whisper from the past, a cryptic message sent from beyond the grave. John realized that the camera itself was a vessel of secrets, a silent witness to the events that had led to his sister's disappearance. The camera held the potential to unlock a door to the past, to reveal the truth that had been hidden for so long.

John's gaze moved from the shadowy figure to Sarah's

face. Her smile was frozen in time, a bittersweet reminder of the life that had been stolen. Her eyes, usually bright and full of life, were obscured by the blurry lens, hidden behind a veil of mystery.

The photograph, a ghostly testament to Sarah's final moments, became John's obsession. He felt an almost physical connection to the image, as if it held a piece of his sister's soul. He spent countless hours studying the photo, tracing the lines of the figure, searching for any detail that might reveal its identity. He imagined the scene captured in the image, the setting, the sounds, the smells, trying to recreate the atmosphere of Sarah's final moments.

The image, though blurry and incomplete, held a power that John could not ignore. It was a key to unlocking the secrets of the past, to finding the truth that had been concealed for so long. The camera, with its single, faded photograph, became the focal point of John's investigation, a silent guide leading him through the labyrinth of memory and deception.

He knew that finding the truth would be a long and arduous journey, fraught with danger and uncertainty. But he was determined, driven by a love for his sister that burned as brightly as the image of her smile in his mind. The camera's secrets would be unveiled, and justice, long denied, would finally be served.

The photograph was a cruel reminder of the day Sarah disappeared. The grainy image, captured by a vintage camera found clutched in the skeletal hand of a long-lost soul, revealed a fleeting glimpse of the past. Sarah's face, youthful and vibrant, was framed by the overgrown bushes of the park. The camera's lens, frozen in time, captured a moment that had become forever etched in John's mind.

He studied the image, his gaze fixated on the edges of the photo, where a shadowy figure lurked in the periphery. The figure was a mere silhouette, obscured by the blurry edges of the image, but John felt a prickling sensation along his spine, a sense of familiarity that sent a chill down his body. He squinted, trying to decipher the outline, searching for any detail, any clue that might unlock the mystery of his sister's disappearance. It was as if the photo, like a forgotten memory, was whispering secrets to him, secrets that he had spent years trying to forget.

The photograph, a ghostly testament to Sarah's final moments, had become the central piece of evidence in a chilling investigation. The blurry image, a haunting reminder of the unsolved case that had haunted John for decades, reignited a desperate search for answers. His heart pounded in his chest, a drumbeat of grief and determination as he examined every detail, every smudge and blur, seeking a clue, a lifeline in the sea of unanswered questions.

John traced the outline of the shadowy figure with his index finger, the cold plastic of the photograph reflecting his own tense face. He closed his eyes, and memories flooded back, memories of his sister, memories of that fateful day, memories that he had tried to bury deep within the recesses of his mind.

He could almost hear her laughter, her voice, a melody that now echoed in his mind as a haunting reminder of her absence. He saw her face, her smile, a radiant glow that had vanished from his life, leaving only a painful void. He could visualize the park, the familiar playground, the sandbox where they used to play, the oak tree that had been their hiding spot. It was a scene that was forever imprinted in his memory, a scene that had been forever tainted by tragedy.

The weight of Sarah's unsolved case pressed down on him, a crushing burden that he had carried for far too long. The passage of time had not diminished the pain, the anger, the yearning for justice. The memories of her disappearance, vivid and agonizing, replayed in his mind like a broken record, each loop a reminder of the unanswered questions, the unresolved grief. The torment of not knowing what had happened to her, who had taken her from him, gnawed at his soul, a constant reminder of his failure to protect her, to bring her home.

John could see it all: the afternoon sun casting long shadows on the park, the sound of children's laughter, Sarah's cheerful voice, the sudden silence that had descended upon the playground, the growing fear in his heart as he realized she was gone. He saw himself running through the park, his heart pounding, his voice hoarse with terror, calling out for her, his desperate pleas echoing through the empty space.

It was a day that had scarred him, a day that had forever changed his life. The shadow of that day, the fear, the guilt, the agony of her absence, had followed him ever since, a persistent reminder of his loss. He had searched for answers, relentlessly pursuing every lead, every possible explanation, only to be met with dead ends and frustrating silences. He had confronted the suspects, interrogated witnesses, dissected evidence, all in a desperate bid to understand, to know, to find the truth.

The passage of time had not brought him any closer to finding out what had happened to Sarah. But the photograph, the only tangible clue to her fate, had awakened something within him, a flicker of hope that had been extinguished long ago. The image was a whisper from the past, a cryptic message that hinted at the truth, a truth that had been hidden in the shadows for decades. John knew that this photograph, this blurry glimpse of the past, might be the key to unlocking the secrets of Sarah's disappearance, to finally bringing her story to a close.

He was determined to find answers, to unravel the truth, even if it meant facing the most horrifying of possibilities. He knew that the path ahead would be fraught with danger, filled with obstacles and deception. But he was willing to face the darkness, to confront his demons, to chase the shadows that had haunted him for years, all for the sake of justice, for the sake of his sister, for the sake of her memory. The photograph, a haunting testament to

Sarah's final moments, would be his guide, his compass, his relentless pursuit of the truth. He would not rest until he found the answer, until he brought her killer to justice, until he found peace.

John's thoughts drifted back to the day Sarah vanished. It was a humid summer afternoon, the air thick with the scent of honeysuckle and the buzz of cicadas. Sarah, all of sixteen, was supposed to be at a friend's house, but she never came home. The phone calls, the frantic searching, the crushing weight of helplessness. Each memory was a sharp shard of pain, piercing the numbness that had settled over his heart.

As the years turned into decades, John had built a life around the void Sarah's absence had created. He channeled his grief into his work, becoming a detective, a relentless pursuer of truth, a silent vow to find justice for his sister. But even with his success, the shadow of the past never fully lifted.

The newly discovered skeleton, clutching a vintage camera, brought a sliver of hope, a flicker of light in the darkness. The photo within the camera, a blurry, fleeting glimpse of a moment frozen in time, held the key to Sarah's fate. He saw a shadowy figure, a man with broad shoulders and a glimpse of a tattoo on his wrist, lurking behind Sarah. The sight sent a jolt of recognition through him.

John was haunted by the memory of a man who had been a frequent visitor at their house during Sarah's childhood. His name was Michael, a family friend who had disappeared from their lives shortly after Sarah's disappearance. Michael was a quiet, almost somber man, a stark contrast to the warmth and exuberance that permeated their family gatherings. John remembered feeling uncomfortable around him, a sense of unease that lingered in the air like a thick fog.

He remembered Michael's presence on that fateful day, the day Sarah vanished. He was sitting on the porch, sipping lemonade, watching Sarah and her friends play in the backyard. John remembered noticing a strange intensity in his gaze, a fixed focus on Sarah that felt unnerving. Michael had left shortly after Sarah disappeared, leaving behind a chilling silence that lingered long after he was gone.

John's investigation led him to the address Michael had given to their parents before his departure. The house, a modest bungalow with a faded paint job and a lawn that needed tending, felt eerily familiar. As he stood on the porch, he could almost hear the echoes of their laughter, the sound of Sarah's voice calling out to her friends, the warmth of the summer sun that had once bathed this house in its golden glow.

He rang the doorbell, his hand trembling slightly. The sound echoed through the silent house, a jarring intrusion into the stillness. The door creaked open, revealing a man who looked older, wearier than he remembered. Michael's eyes, once bright and filled with a quiet intensity, were now shadowed with a deep melancholy, a heavy weight of unspoken emotions that he couldn't shake.

"John," Michael whispered, his voice raspy and low, as if he hadn't spoken in years. "I've been waiting for you. I knew you'd come."

John felt a cold shiver run down his spine. The weight of the past, the heavy shroud of Sarah's unsolved disappearance, seemed to press down on him, suffocating him with its suffocating grip.

"What do you mean?" John asked, his voice tight with tension. "What do you know?"

Michael stepped aside, inviting John into the house. The air inside was heavy, thick with the scent of dust and neglect. The furniture was covered in sheets, and the windows were shrouded in darkness. The house felt frozen in time, a mausoleum of memories where the ghosts of the past lingered.

John noticed a framed photograph on the mantelpiece, a faded image of a younger Michael, his face beaming with a youthful energy. The smile was strained, forced, as if he were trying to mask something, a secret buried deep within him.

"I remember that day," Michael said, his voice a strained whisper. "The day Sarah disappeared. I remember everything. I was here, I was watching, I was... I was..." He trailed off, his voice dissolving into a choked sob.

John moved closer to Michael, feeling a surge of empathy for the man he had once seen as a friend. "What happened?" he asked gently. "What did you see?"

Michael looked up at John, his eyes filled with pain and regret. "I saw her leave the house," he said, his voice trembling. "She was angry, upset. She ran out the back door, she was crying, she said she was going to find a place where no one could find her."

John felt a wave of confusion wash over him. Sarah had never been known for her impulsiveness. Her actions on that day didn't fit her personality, her demeanor. Why had she run away? What had happened to make her so angry?

"What happened to her?" John asked, his voice laced with desperation. "What happened to my sister?"

Michael's face twisted in anguish, his shoulders shaking with a deep, guttural sob. "I don't know," he whispered, his voice barely audible. "I saw her go. I saw her leave, and then I never saw her again."

John felt a sudden wave of suspicion, a prickling sensation of unease that he couldn't shake. Michael's story, his emotional breakdown, the way he seemed to be both haunted and haunted by Sarah's disappearance, all raised red flags. He knew that the truth was not as simple as Michael was making it seem.

"What were you doing here?" John asked, his voice firm,

laced with a newfound suspicion. "Why were you watching Sarah?"

Michael looked at John, his eyes filled with a mixture of fear and defiance. "I was just… I was just a friend. I cared about her. I wanted to make sure she was okay."

John felt a surge of anger mixed with a deep sense of frustration. He knew that Michael was not being honest, that he was hiding something. The questions piled up, the suspicions grew. The shadow of doubt crept into the crevices of his mind, casting a dark pall over the already somber mood.

"Where were you after Sarah left the house?" John pressed, his voice unwavering. "What did you do next? Where did you go? Tell me the truth, Michael."

Michael's face tightened, his eyes darting nervously from side to side. "I… I don't know. I don't remember. It was a long time ago," he said, his voice wavering.

John knew that Michael was lying. The way he looked at him, the way he was struggling to maintain his composure, the fear in his eyes, all told him that he knew more than he was willing to admit. He knew that Michael was a suspect, a potential link to Sarah's disappearance, and he was determined to unravel the truth, no matter how painful it might be.

John spent the next few days digging into Michael's past, searching for any clues that might lead him to Sarah. He interviewed Michael's former neighbors, classmates, and colleagues, trying to piece together a picture of the man who had been a fixture in their lives for so long.

He discovered that Michael had a history of impulsive behavior, a reckless streak that had led him into trouble on numerous occasions. He had been arrested for driving under the influence, for fighting, and for vandalism. He had also been accused of stealing from his family and friends, but the charges had never been proven.

John's investigation led him to a local bar where Michael had frequented, a place where he had spent countless hours drinking and gambling. He spoke to the bartender, who described Michael as a heavy drinker who could get violent when he was intoxicated.

The bartender described an incident where Michael had gotten into a brawl with another patron. The other patron had been injured, and Michael had fled the scene. The bartender said he had never seen Michael in the bar again after that night.

John pieced together a chilling portrait of a troubled man, a man who was capable of violence and deception. The more he learned about Michael, the more his suspicions grew. He knew that Michael had to be connected to Sarah's disappearance, that he had to know more than he was letting on.

He was determined to find out what he had seen, what he had done, and what he was hiding. He knew that the truth was out there, buried beneath layers of lies and deception, and he was going to find it, even if it meant tearing Michael's world apart.

John's investigation led him to the Snider family's history, a history filled with both love and conflict. He spoke to his parents, his voice heavy with emotion, as he tried to understand what had transpired years ago. The conversation was a painful dance, filled with silences and guarded responses. John learned that Sarah, the carefree spirit he remembered, had a turbulent relationship with their parents, their differences often erupting into heated arguments.

His parents revealed that Sarah's rebellious nature, her yearning for independence, and her penchant for breaking the rules, had always strained their relationship. They spoke of her defiant streak, her desire to carve her own path, and how she had often clashed with their conservative values. Sarah, they said, had a fire in her eyes, a yearning for adventure that often took her to places they couldn't comprehend. They had tried to guide her, to steer her back to what they considered the right path, but their efforts often met with resistance.

John delved deeper, uncovering instances where Sarah had defied their wishes, engaging in activities they disapproved of. She had dropped out of college, much to their dismay, choosing to pursue her passion for photography, a path they believed was unstable and unpromising. She had taken impulsive road trips, leaving them with unanswered calls and worries about her safety. Her independent spirit had pushed her to make choices that clashed with their expectations, creating a chasm between them.

As John pieced together the fragments of their past, he discovered a deep-seated resentment simmering beneath the surface. His parents, while professing their love for Sarah, couldn't hide the underlying disappointment and frustration they felt. They spoke of her recklessness, her carelessness, and how her choices had caused them endless worry.

But there were whispers, snippets of information that hinted at something more. They talked about an incident, a confrontation that had shaken them to their core. Sarah, they said, had been accused of something, an accusation that had left them reeling and shattered their trust in her. The details were vague, shrouded in secrecy, but the weight of their words revealed a deep wound, a chasm that had never healed.

John pressed, eager for answers, but his parents remained tight-lipped. They refused to reveal the details of the accusation, claiming it was a private matter, a painful memory they wished to bury. Their reluctance, their guarded expressions, only fueled John's suspicions. He felt a cold dread creep into his heart. Could Sarah's rebellious streak, her defiance of her parents, have made her an enemy? Had she been entangled in something that had ultimately led to her disappearance?

John's investigation led him to Sarah's friends, hoping to

gain a different perspective on their shared past. They painted a different picture, a portrait of a vibrant, free-spirited young woman who lived life on her own terms. They spoke of Sarah's passion for photography, her love of music, and her adventurous spirit. They told of her captivating smile, her kind heart, and her ability to make friends wherever she went.

However, their stories also revealed a darker side. They spoke of Sarah's tumultuous relationships, the heartbreak she had endured, and the emotional scars that lingered beneath her confident façade. They told of a troubled romance, a relationship that had ended badly, leaving Sarah in a state of turmoil.

They whispered of a man, a mysterious figure who had appeared in Sarah's life, a man who had charmed her and then betrayed her trust. This man, they said, had been manipulative and possessive, and his actions had left Sarah shattered and emotionally drained. They hinted at secrets, whispers of something more sinister, but they refused to elaborate, citing a fear of retaliation and a desire to protect their friend.

John felt a knot tightening in his stomach. The pieces were slowly falling into place, forming a disturbing picture. Sarah's rebellious streak, her tumultuous relationships, and her penchant for taking risks had put her in harm's way. The accusation his parents had hinted at, the mysterious man they had refused to discuss, and the secrets her friends refused to reveal all pointed towards a possible motive, a reason for someone to want her gone.

John couldn't shake the feeling that there was a connection between Sarah's family, her friends, and the shadowy figure that lurked in the background of the photograph. The lines between suspicion and truth were becoming increasingly blurred, leaving him lost in a labyrinth of unanswered questions.

Chapter 2: The Glimmer of Hope

John meticulously examined the blurry photograph, his brow furrowed in concentration. He had spent countless hours poring over every detail, trying to decipher the faint outlines of the figure lurking in the shadows behind Sarah. There was something, a detail that had eluded him until now. His eyes landed on the killer's wrist, where a faint outline of a tattoo emerged from the grainy image. It was a small, intricate design, a symbol of a unique kind. This was his missing link, the key that could unlock the mystery.

A wave of hope surged through John. He knew he had to find someone who could translate the tattoo into a tangible piece of evidence, a visual representation that could lead him to the killer's identity. He had heard whispers of a renowned forensic artist, a woman with an almost supernatural ability to reconstruct faces from the faintest of clues. She had a reputation for being meticulous, dedicated, and incredibly skilled in her craft. John was determined to find her.

He contacted the artist, a woman named Evelyn, and explained his situation. He showed her the photograph, pointing out the tattoo and emphasizing its significance. Evelyn listened intently, her gaze focused on the image. She understood the importance of this single clue, the weight of the mystery it held. She knew that the tattoo could be the key to solving a case that had remained unsolved for 25 years.

Evelyn spent hours studying the photograph, carefully analyzing every detail. She noted the angle of the killer's wrist, the position of the tattoo, and the intricate details that could be gleaned from the blurred image. She meticulously sketched the tattoo, recreating its design with precision and accuracy. She then began the painstaking process of building a composite sketch, using the photograph as a guide and integrating the tattoo into the killer's appearance.

As Evelyn worked, John observed her with a mixture of anticipation and trepidation. He hoped that she could create a sketch that would be recognizable, that would help him track down the person responsible for Sarah's disappearance. He knew that it was a long shot, but he clung to the glimmer of hope that this sketch could be the key to finding his sister's killer.

Days turned into weeks as Evelyn worked on the composite sketch. She spent countless hours staring at the photograph, her mind filled with the faces of countless suspects, the memories of countless crimes. She had honed her skills over years of experience, becoming a master of her craft, but this case was different. This case held a weight, a significance that transcended the usual demands of her profession. It was a chance to bring closure to a family that had been haunted by tragedy for too long.

Finally, Evelyn presented John with the completed sketch. It was a chillingly accurate depiction, a reconstruction of the killer's face based on the photograph and the tattoo. The sketch captured the essence of the figure lurking in the shadows, bringing the killer's face to life. It was a ghostly apparition, a haunting image that filled John with a mix of emotions – dread, determination, and a flicker of hope.

John stared at the sketch, the image imprinted in his mind. He knew that this was his chance to finally bring Sarah's killer to justice. He had spent 25 years haunted by her disappearance, consumed by a need to find answers. He had searched for clues, followed leads, and faced the weight of his own grief. Now, he had a face, a name, a potential path to closure. He would not let this opportunity slip away.

John thanked Evelyn profusely, promising to keep her updated on his progress. He knew that he would need her help as he delved deeper into the investigation, but for now, he was focused on the immediate task at hand. He had a face, a possible lead, and a renewed sense of purpose. He was going to find his sister's killer, no matter what.

John's focus shifted to the sketch. He studied it intently, his mind piecing together the details. The artist had captured the essence of the figure in the photograph, highlighting the unique tattoo on the wrist. It was a small, intricate design, a swirling pattern that resembled a vine with a single, delicate rose at its center.

John felt a familiar pang of unease as he examined the sketch. It seemed to whisper secrets, revealing a hidden world that he had never known before. He remembered his father's words, the ones he had uttered years ago, about a family secret that had been kept for generations. A secret that had cost them dearly.

The detective followed the trail of the tattoo, tracing it back to the city's underbelly, a labyrinth of hidden alleys and dimly lit bars. His inquiries led him to a woman named Emily, a woman who had known Sarah as a child. They had been close friends, sharing secrets and dreams, until their paths diverged.

Emily was now a ghost, a shadow of her former self, her eyes filled with a haunted sorrow. She had been a recluse for years, retreating from the world, seeking solace in the memories of a past that had faded.

"Emily," John spoke softly, his voice hesitant as he approached her, "I need your help. I'm looking for answers about Sarah's disappearance. I believe you might know something."

Emily's gaze was cold and distant, her eyes reflecting a lifetime of pain and sorrow. "Why should I help you?" she asked, her voice a hollow echo.

"Because Sarah was your friend. And because I believe you know something that could help me find her."

Emily turned away, her voice a whisper. "Sarah and I...we had a falling out. Years ago, before she went missing. We haven't spoken in a long time."

John pressed further, his intuition telling him that Emily was hiding something. "What happened, Emily? What was the falling out about?"

Emily hesitated, her memories flickering like dying embers. "It was a stupid fight," she finally admitted, her voice heavy with regret. "It was a misunderstanding. We were young and foolish. But it left deep scars, scars that never truly healed."

John urged her to tell him more. He knew that the past held the key to the present, that the secrets buried beneath the surface would reveal the truth. He had to learn what had happened between Sarah and Emily, what had driven them apart, what secrets they had shared.

Emily's story unfolded like a tapestry of pain and resentment. It was a story of betrayal, of a broken friendship, and of a deep-seated anger that had lingered for years.

"Sarah took something from me," she confessed, her eyes filled with a bitter hatred. "She took something that I loved, something that I had held onto for so long."

John pressed for details, wanting to understand what had happened. "What did she take from you, Emily? What did you love that she took?"

"She took him," Emily whispered, her voice barely audible. "He was mine. He loved me. But Sarah stole him away from me. She stole his heart and his love."

John's heart sank as he realized the depth of Emily's resentment. He now understood the source of her anger, the pain that had been festering for years. But he still didn't understand the connection to Sarah's disappearance.

"Emily," he pleaded, "Please tell me more. What happened? What happened to him? And what does it have to do with Sarah's disappearance?"

Emily's gaze fell to the floor, her body trembling with the weight of her memories. "He was a photographer," she said, her voice barely above a whisper. "He was talented, brilliant. And he loved me. But Sarah...she was different. She was alluring, mysterious. She had a power that I could never compete with."

John listened intently, his mind racing as Emily's story unfolded. The name of the photographer, the one who had stolen Emily's heart and her love, was David. He was a talented photographer, a man who captured the essence of his subjects, who saw the beauty within them. But there was a darkness within him, a shadow side that had been hidden for years.

"David...he was the one who took the photos of Sarah, the ones that were found with the skeleton?" John asked, his voice filled with a growing sense of dread.

Emily nodded, her eyes filled with a chilling sadness. "He was obsessed with Sarah. He followed her, photographed her, captured her every move. He wanted to own her, to possess her. But Sarah...she didn't want him. She rejected him. And he couldn't handle it."

"Emily, what happened to David?" John asked, his voice edged with urgency. "Where is he now? Is he the one who took Sarah?"

Emily's gaze shifted, her eyes avoiding John's. "I don't know," she whispered, her voice trembling. "I haven't seen him in years. He disappeared after...after what happened to Sarah."

John's instincts screamed at him. He knew that Emily was holding back, that she was hiding something. But he also knew that she was scared, terrified of the darkness she had witnessed, of the secret she had carried for so long.

"Emily," he pleaded, "I need your help. I need to know what happened to Sarah. I need to know what happened to David. Please, I beg you, tell me everything you know."

Emily stared at him, her eyes filled with a mix of fear and defiance. "I can't tell you," she said, her voice a choked whisper. "It's too dangerous. I'm afraid. I'm afraid of what might happen to me."

John knew he couldn't force her. He had to find another way, a way to break through the wall of fear that she had built around herself. He had to convince her that he was on her side, that he wanted to help her, not hurt her.

"I understand your fear, Emily," he said, his voice gentle

and reassuring. "But I promise you, I'm not here to harm you. I'm here to help you. I'm here to find the truth, and I believe you are the only one who can help me."

John reached out, his hand hovering over Emily's. He felt a connection to her, a sense of shared sorrow and a desperate need to find answers.

"Please, Emily," he pleaded. "For Sarah's sake. For your sake. Tell me what you know."

Emily hesitated, her eyes meeting John's. She saw the sincerity in his gaze, the desperation in his voice. She knew that he was truly trying to help her, to find the truth.

"Okay," she whispered, her voice a broken melody. "I'll tell you. But you have to promise me you'll be careful. He's dangerous. He's a monster."

John nodded, his heart pounding with anticipation. He was finally getting close to the truth, to the answers he had been searching for for years.

Emily's voice grew stronger as she recounted the events leading up to Sarah's disappearance. She told John about David's obsession with Sarah, about the photographs he had taken, about the way he had watched her, followed her, stalked her.

"He was obsessed with her," Emily said, her voice filled with a chilling dread. "He was obsessed with capturing her, with possessing her. He couldn't handle the fact that she didn't want him. He couldn't handle the rejection."

Emily told John how David had confronted Sarah one night, in a secluded spot where he had often photographed her. She had tried to reason with him, to tell him to leave her alone. But David had lost control. He had become enraged, and in a moment of blind fury, he had lashed out.

"He hurt her," Emily whispered, her voice choked with emotion. "He hurt her badly. I saw it. I was there. I watched it happen. I couldn't stop him."

John listened, his mind reeling. He was now piecing together the puzzle, seeing the pieces fall into place. David was the killer, the monster who had taken Sarah from him. But why? What was his motive?

"Emily," he asked, his voice filled with a desperate need for understanding. "What happened to Sarah? What did he do to her?"

Emily's eyes filled with tears, the pain of her memories washing over her. "He...he took her," she whispered. "He took her to a place where he often photographed her. A place where he could be alone with her, where he could control her, where he could own her. He never let her go."

John's heart pounded in his chest. He knew that he had to find David, to bring him to justice, to avenge Sarah. He had to find the place where David had taken Sarah, the place where he had left her, the place where she had been hidden for all these years.

"Emily," John said, his voice filled with a steely determination. "Where did he take her? Where is she now?"

Emily's voice was barely a whisper, her fear palpable. "He...he took her to the old mill," she said, her voice cracking with emotion. "The one by the river. He always photographed her there. He said it was a special place, a place where he could feel close to her."

John thanked Emily, his mind racing with the new information. He knew he had to act quickly. David was a dangerous man, and he was still out there, free to hurt others.

John rushed out of Emily's apartment, his mind set on the old mill. He knew that this was the place where he would find Sarah, the place where he would confront David, the place where he would finally bring his sister's killer to justice.

John had spent weeks poring over the blurry photograph, meticulously examining every detail. The photograph had become his obsession, a single glimpse into his sister's final moments. It was a ghostly reminder of Sarah's disappearance, a faded image that held the key to unraveling the truth.

He had identified a small, unique tattoo on the killer's wrist, a distinguishing feature that could be the missing piece of the puzzle. The tattoo, barely visible in the blurry photo, was a distinctive symbol – a stylized crescent moon with a star embedded in its center.

With the tattoo as a lead, John had sought the help of a renowned forensic artist, a master of recreating faces from fragmented memories. Together, they had poured over the photograph, dissecting every shadow and line, painstakingly crafting a composite sketch based on the photograph and the tattoo.

The sketch, a ghostly echo of the killer's face, revealed a woman with a sharp jawline, piercing eyes, and a determined expression. She had a certain aura of mystery, a sense of hidden secrets that sent shivers down John's spine.

John's investigation led him to Emily, a woman who had known Sarah during their childhood. Emily was a distant acquaintance, a figure from Sarah's past that had faded from their lives. He had only a few fleeting memories of her, but she had always remained a presence in the background, a shadowy figure from Sarah's youth.

As John delved deeper into Emily's life, he discovered that she had a complex history with Sarah. Their relationship had been strained, marked by a deep resentment that Emily had carefully hidden. John learned of an event from their childhood, a moment that had irrevocably damaged their friendship.

Sarah, always the outgoing and adventurous one, had led Emily into a dangerous situation, a reckless act of youthful defiance. The incident, which had resulted in a minor injury for Emily, had left her with a deep bitterness towards Sarah, a resentment that had festered over the years.

John's investigation revealed that Emily had been harboring a secret, a long-held grudge that had fueled her desire to see Sarah gone. Her motive, though veiled in layers of denial and self-preservation, became increasingly clear as John dug deeper.

However, John struggled to find concrete evidence against Emily. Her alibi for the day of Sarah's disappearance was airtight, supported by a series of seemingly unrelated events. She had meticulously crafted a narrative, weaving a tapestry of lies that seemed to corroborate her story.

Despite the lack of concrete evidence, John couldn't shake the feeling that Emily was hiding something. Her demeanor was guarded, her answers evasive, and her eyes held a chilling intensity that sent a cold shiver down John's spine.

He discovered that Emily had been in contact with Sarah on the day of her disappearance, their last conversation a brief exchange of messages that spoke of a strained relationship, a simmering resentment. The messages were innocuous, offering no concrete proof of wrongdoing, but they suggested a deeper connection, a lingering tension that hinted at a hidden conflict.

John's intuition whispered that Emily was more than just a disgruntled acquaintance. She was a woman with a dark secret, a hidden agenda that he was determined to uncover. His pursuit of justice was fueled by a gut instinct, a belief that Emily held the key to unlocking the truth.

His investigation led him to Emily's apartment, a small, cluttered space filled with faded photographs and dusty mementos. He carefully examined the photographs, searching for clues, for any telltale signs of her involvement in Sarah's disappearance.

Among the dusty photographs, John found a particular picture that caught his attention. It was a faded snapshot of Sarah, taken during a family vacation years ago. The photo itself was unremarkable, but it was the object tucked behind the frame that sent a jolt of adrenaline through John's veins.

It was a small, silver necklace, intricately designed with a delicate crescent moon and a star embedded within its center. The necklace was strikingly similar to the tattoo on the killer's wrist, a chilling coincidence that sent a wave of suspicion through John.

John's heart pounded in his chest as he realized the significance of his discovery. It was a piece of evidence, a tangible link between Emily and the crime. The necklace, a forgotten memory, a silent testament to her involvement.

He confronted Emily with the necklace, questioning her about its origins. She stammered, her eyes darting nervously as she struggled to explain the unexpected find. Her voice, usually calm and measured, trembled with a hint of panic, betraying her composure.

Emily vehemently denied any involvement in Sarah's disappearance. She claimed she had no memory of the necklace, claiming it was a lost relic from her youth, a forgotten trinket from a past she had long forgotten. Her explanation was plausible, her words convincing, but John couldn't shake his doubts.

He pressed on, demanding answers, his questions growing more pointed with each passing moment. Emily, cornered and desperate, began to unravel. She admitted to having a strained relationship with Sarah, a past that had been marked by resentment and bitterness.

However, she insisted she had nothing to do with Sarah's disappearance, claiming she had been framed, her life tainted by a conspiracy she couldn't explain. Her words were a mix of truth and deceit, a performance carefully crafted to distract and deflect.

John, caught in a web of lies and deception, was left with more questions than answers. He couldn't ignore the evidence, the undeniable connection between Emily and the necklace, but he also recognized the possibility that he was being misled. He had to tread carefully, separating truth from fabricated stories, navigating a treacherous path that could lead him to the truth or to a dead end.

He knew that he couldn't trust Emily's words, that her story was a carefully constructed façade. He needed to dig deeper, to uncover the truth hidden beneath layers of deception. The quest for justice, for his sister's memory, was far from over.

John felt a familiar pang of unease as he stared at Emily's photo. There was a stillness in her eyes that didn't quite match the vibrant girl he remembered from their shared childhood. He recalled her laughter, her mischievous grin, and the way she'd always been the life of the party, but now, all he saw was a chilling emptiness. The photograph captured a fleeting moment, a glimpse of a woman who seemed to be carrying a heavy secret.

He had to know more. John's fingers traced the lines of the composite sketch, focusing on the details that the forensic artist had painstakingly drawn. He imagined the tattoo, a faded symbol of a wolf howling at the moon, etched onto Emily's wrist. The wolf, a creature of the night, seemed to echo the darkness that John sensed in Emily's eyes.

It was time to dig deeper. John had spent weeks scrutinizing Sarah's belongings, combing through her personal diaries and journals, searching for clues that might illuminate the secrets of her disappearance. He had found nothing substantial, nothing that could tie her to Emily, but he knew the photo held a truth that he had to uncover. He spent hours examining the details, the shadows, the slight tilt of Emily's head, the subtle shift in her expression. Each detail felt significant, each nuance whispered a story that John felt compelled to decipher.

He started with the jewelry. Sarah had a penchant for collecting unique pieces, often finding treasures at antique shops and flea markets. She had a particular fondness for a delicate silver pendant shaped like a crescent moon, adorned with a small amethyst stone. John remembered how she'd always worn it, nestled against her heart, as if it held a secret within its silvery embrace.

He carefully searched through Emily's belongings, meticulously sifting through her drawers, her closet, her desk, his heart pounding with every item he touched. It was a delicate dance, a desperate search for a piece of the puzzle, a shard of truth that might connect Emily to the events of Sarah's disappearance. He felt a tremor of hope when his fingers brushed against a velvet box tucked away in a corner of Emily's desk drawer. He lifted the lid, his breath catching in his throat. Inside lay the silver crescent moon pendant, its amethyst stone glinting under the dim light of his desk lamp.

The pendant was unmistakable, a piece of Sarah's heart, a tangible link to the past. Its presence in Emily's belongings was a bombshell, a jarring revelation that shattered the fragile hope John had clung to. He found himself staring at the pendant, its silver surface reflecting the weight of the truth he had just unearthed. It was a piece of evidence, a tangible manifestation of the secrets that Emily had been guarding for years.

The discovery of the pendant sparked a whirlwind of emotions within John. A wave of anger washed over him, a burning desire for justice for his sister. He felt the weight of her disappearance, the emptiness that had haunted him for years, growing heavier with every passing moment. He needed answers, he needed to know the truth, and he was determined to uncover it, even if it meant facing the darkest corners of Emily's past.

John knew that this discovery was only the beginning. He needed to connect the dots, to understand the significance of the pendant, and to unravel the web of deceit that Emily had woven around herself. He had to know why she had taken Sarah's pendant, why she had kept it hidden for so long, and what role, if any, she had played in Sarah's disappearance.

He traced the outline of the crescent moon pendant with his fingertips, its silver surface cool and smooth against his skin. He could feel the weight of Sarah's memory, the echoes of her laughter, the whisper of her secrets, clinging to the pendant's surface. He knew that he had to follow the trail, to follow the clues, and to uncover the truth.

John felt a surge of determination. He wouldn't let Emily's deceit, her carefully constructed facade, stand in his way. He wouldn't rest until he had pieced together the puzzle, until he had revealed the truth that had been buried for so long. He had to understand the events that had led to Sarah's disappearance, to understand the motives of those involved, to understand the darkness that had consumed his sister's life and left him forever scarred.

He knew that the journey ahead would be perilous, filled with twists and turns, and the possibility of facing the truth might be more terrifying than he could imagine. But he was determined, driven by a burning desire for justice, fueled by the love he had for his sister, and the promise he had made to her, a promise he would never break.

The pendant, a silent witness, had whispered its secrets, revealing a truth that John had long suspected. The pieces were starting to fall into place, and he was determined to unearth the truth, no matter the cost. The search for Sarah had led him down a dark and twisted path, a path he had to follow to the very end.

As he stared at the pendant, the weight of his sister's absence, the mystery of her disappearance, and the chilling possibilities that Emily's possession of the pendant presented, weighed heavily on his heart. But he wouldn't let fear paralyze him. He wouldn't let the shadows of the past consume him. He had to move forward, he had to follow the trail, and he had to find the answers he so desperately sought.

He knew the path ahead would be filled with obstacles, with betrayals, and with the possibility of facing truths that might shatter his world. But he had come too far to turn back. His sister's memory, her unspoken plea for justice, drove him forward. He had to find the truth, no matter the cost, and he would not rest until he had found it.

The air in the small, cluttered office was thick with tension. John, his face grim, slammed a small, ornate box onto Emily's desk. He'd been tracking her for weeks, piecing together the fragments of her past, and each piece seemed to point in the same direction. He felt a tremor of anger course through him as he stared at the delicate silver pendant resting inside the box. It was a familiar sight – the same pendant Sarah had worn on the day she vanished.

Emily's eyes widened as she recognized the pendant, her composure crumbling ever so slightly. "This... This is absurd," she stammered, her voice a shaky whisper. "I don't know how this got here."

John crossed his arms, his gaze unwavering. "You deny any involvement in Sarah's disappearance, yet here we have a piece of her jewelry found in your possession." He pulled out a photograph, the grainy image of the composite sketch he'd had made based on the blurry picture from the vintage camera. "And let's not forget this. The artist was able to identify a unique tattoo on the killer's wrist. A tattoo you have, Emily."

Her face went pale, and she clutched the desk, trying to maintain a semblance of control. "I told you, I was framed. Someone planted this on me, someone who wants to see me suffer. Someone who wants to see me pay for something I didn't do."

"Is that so?" John scoffed, his voice laced with skepticism. "You seem to have an uncanny knack for being in the wrong place at the wrong time. You were at the carnival that day, remember? The same carnival where Sarah was last seen."

"Coincidence," she insisted, her voice rising a notch. "I was just there with a friend. We spent the day riding rides and eating cotton candy. It was a completely normal day. A day that has been twisted and manipulated by someone who wants to see me fall."

John knew he couldn't trust her words, not anymore. Every fiber of his being screamed that she was hiding something, that she was the key to unraveling the mystery that had haunted him for decades. The pendant, the tattoo, her presence at the carnival – all these pieces fit together, forming a disturbing picture that he couldn't ignore.

"You knew Sarah, Emily. You were friends with her. You knew how close she was to our family. So, tell me, why would someone frame you for her disappearance?"

"It's all a lie!" she shouted, her voice thick with emotion. "I'm not the one you should be chasing. You need to talk to Michael. He was the one who was obsessed with Sarah, who was jealous of her relationship with our family. He was the one who was always lurking in the shadows, watching her."

John's mind raced, trying to reconcile her words with the evidence he had gathered. Michael, a childhood friend of Sarah's, had always seemed harmless, even shy. But there was a flicker of doubt, a seed of suspicion planted in John's mind. He had dismissed Michael as a potential suspect in the past, convinced that his gentle demeanor couldn't hide a dark secret. But Emily's accusations, however unlikely they seemed, offered a new perspective.

John pushed back from his desk, his gaze meeting Emily's defiant stare. "You have a lot to answer for, Emily. But I'm not done with you yet." He turned, his footsteps echoing in the quiet office as he left.

He needed to find Michael, to hear his side of the story. He needed to find out the truth, no matter how painful or disturbing it might be. The possibility that Michael, someone he once considered a friend, was capable of such a heinous act sent a shiver down his spine.

John knew he had to be careful. Emily's claims could be a ploy to distract him, to shift the blame away from herself. He needed to tread carefully, to separate truth from fabrication, to uncover the web of deceit that seemed to be woven around Sarah's disappearance.

He had a nagging feeling that the truth was closer than he thought, lurking just beneath the surface, waiting to be exposed. The pressure was mounting, the weight of the investigation bearing down on him. He had to find answers, not just for his sister, but for himself, to finally find peace after years of agonizing uncertainty.

The drive to Michael's house was a blur of anxious

thoughts. The once-familiar road, lined with sprawling houses and manicured lawns, now felt ominous, charged with a dark energy that mirrored the turmoil in John's mind. He parked his car in the driveway, the silence of the neighborhood punctuated only by the chirping of crickets.

He walked up to the front door, a sense of apprehension growing with every step. He remembered Michael from their childhood, a timid boy with a kind face and a gentle soul. Could that same boy have grown into a man capable of taking a life, of leaving a family heartbroken? He took a deep breath and knocked, the sound echoing in the quiet afternoon.

Moments passed, each one filled with mounting tension. Finally, the door creaked open, revealing Michael's face. His eyes, once filled with a youthful innocence, were now shadowed with a weariness that John recognized as the mark of someone burdened by a heavy secret.

"John," Michael whispered, his voice barely audible. "What are you doing here?"

"I need to talk to you, Michael," John said, his voice firm. "About Sarah. About what happened that day."

The color drained from Michael's face. He stumbled back, his eyes darting around the doorway as if seeking an escape. "I... I don't know what you're talking about. I haven't seen Sarah in years."

John's gaze locked with Michael's. "Don't lie to me, Michael. Emily said you were obsessed with Sarah, that you were jealous of her. She said you were the one who was watching her that day."

The blood drained from Michael's face, replaced by a sickly pallor. He opened his mouth to speak, but the words seemed to catch in his throat, leaving him speechless. His silence spoke volumes, confirming John's worst fears.

"Tell me the truth, Michael," John pleaded. "Tell me what happened to Sarah. We can get through this together."

Michael hesitated, his gaze flickering between John and the closed door behind him. He seemed to be caught in a struggle, torn between the desire to protect himself and the need to confess.

"I… I can't, John. I'm sorry." He swallowed hard, his voice trembling. "It's not… it's not what you think. I was… I was just trying to help her."

John's brow furrowed. "Help her? How? And how could you help her by disappearing with her?"

Michael took a step back, his eyes filled with a mixture of fear and guilt. "I… I can't tell you. It's not safe. Please, John, just go. You need to protect yourself. You need to protect your family." He closed the door, the sound of the latch clicking shut echoing in the silence.

John stood there, his hand frozen on the doorknob, the weight of the world pressing down on him. He felt a sudden surge of anger, but it was quickly replaced by a gnawing sense of dread. He knew he couldn't leave, not without answers. He had to uncover the truth, no matter the cost.

The sun was setting, casting long shadows across the neighborhood. The silence felt oppressive, broken only by the distant sound of a car engine. John turned and walked back to his car, a wave of despair washing over him. He had come seeking answers, but he left with even more questions. The truth, like a phantom, was always just out of reach, taunting him with its elusive presence.

As he drove away, he couldn't shake the feeling that he was being watched. He looked back at the house, but saw only the empty street and the shadows of the trees. The unsettling feeling lingered, a persistent whisper in the back of his mind, reminding him that the danger was always lurking, always close.

Chapter 3: The Killer's Identity

The crisp autumn air bit at John's face as he stood outside the diner, the faded "Open" sign creaking in the wind. He was chasing a new lead, a glimmer of hope in a case that had haunted him for decades. The witness, a middle-aged woman with eyes that held a mix of fear and determination, claimed to have seen Sarah, his sister, and a suspicious-looking man near the location where her body was eventually found. It had been a fleeting glimpse, a blurry image etched in her memory, but it was the first tangible clue he had in years.

"I was driving home from work," the woman, whose name was Mrs. Jenkins, had said, her voice trembling slightly, "it was late, maybe around ten o'clock. I remember it was a cold night, just like tonight. I was on Elm Street, heading towards the old abandoned mill, and I saw them... two figures... standing by the side of the road. I didn't get a good look, but the man... he was tall, wearing a dark coat, and had a thick beard. And he had this... this glint in his eye. I couldn't shake the feeling something was wrong."

John had listened intently, every word echoing in the cramped diner booth. He scribbled down Mrs. Jenkins' description, the details weaving a tapestry of hope and despair. It was a long shot, but this witness could be the missing piece, the link to Sarah's last moments.

"What about the car?" John pressed, his voice a low rumble.

Mrs. Jenkins paused, her brow furrowed in concentration. "It was a dark sedan, old, maybe from the 1970s. It was a bit rusty, but it had this distinct, almost rusted orange, color... I couldn't make out the make or model, but I remember that color, it was like a faded sunset."

John thanked Mrs. Jenkins, his mind swirling with possibilities. The witness's testimony provided a starting point, a direction to follow. He visualized the scene, the two figures silhouetted against the backdrop of the old mill, the eerie glow of the streetlamp illuminating the rusted orange car.

The first stop was the police station, where he retrieved the case files from Sarah's disappearance. Years of dust and neglect covered the thick folders, the pages filled with faded photographs and handwritten notes. He spent hours combing through the evidence, searching for anything that corroborated Mrs. Jenkins' account. The old sketches of potential suspects, the witness statements, the timeline of events, everything was analyzed with renewed urgency.

His search yielded little, but he found a mention of a man named David, a former employee of a local photography studio, who had been dismissed for inappropriate behavior. David's name had appeared briefly in the investigation, a red herring that had been dismissed due to a lack of evidence.

John remembered David, a lanky man with a brooding

presence and a piercing gaze. He had been a dark horse, a fleeting shadow in the investigation. Now, with the witness's description, he was starting to see David in a new light. The rusty orange car, the faded sunset, it all seemed to fit. It was too much of a coincidence.

He drove to the photography studio, the weathered sign creaking in the wind. The owner, a woman with a sharp tongue and a knowing glint in her eyes, confirmed that David had been employed there, but she was reluctant to divulge any details.

"He was a troubled soul," she said, her voice laced with disdain, "he had a way of fixating on things, especially women. He would take pictures without their permission, sometimes following them around. It was unsettling, to say the least. But he never did anything illegal... at least, not that I knew of."

John pressed on, questioning her about David's vehicles. The woman confirmed that he had driven an old, rusty orange car, a beat-up Ford Mustang that seemed to be falling apart. The details matched the witness's description perfectly.

He couldn't shake the feeling that he was closing in on the truth. David, the troubled photographer, the man with a dark side, he was starting to look like the prime suspect. John spent the next few days meticulously tracing David's whereabouts on the night of Sarah's disappearance, a night that had changed his life forever. He spoke to David's neighbors, his coworkers, anyone who could provide a glimpse into his past. The stories were chilling, painting a picture of a man obsessed with Sarah, a man who seemed to be consumed by a dark desire.

He discovered that David had been obsessed with Sarah for years, secretly taking pictures of her without her knowledge. He had followed her, studied her, and become consumed by her. It was a stalker's obsession, a dangerous fascination that had turned deadly.

He found a series of photographs, hidden in David's attic, capturing Sarah at her most vulnerable. They were stolen moments, glimpses into her private life, revealing a chilling pattern of obsession. There were photographs of her walking to work, of her shopping at the grocery store, of her at the park with friends. He had captured her every move, every detail.

The photographs revealed a chilling detail. One photograph, taken near the old mill, captured Sarah standing by the side of the road, looking distressed, her eyes filled with fear. In the background, a dark figure, shrouded in shadows, loomed behind her. It was David. He was the man Mrs. Jenkins had seen, the man who had taken Sarah's life.

Armed with the evidence, John confronted David. The man, now a broken shadow of his former self, confessed to his crimes. He had been obsessed with Sarah, consumed by a desire to possess her. When she refused his advances, he snapped, taking her life in a fit of rage.

The confession brought a bittersweet sense of closure, the weight of years of searching finally lifted. But the pain of Sarah's loss remained, a constant reminder of the tragedy that had consumed his life. John spent countless hours revisiting the crime scene, the abandoned mill where his sister's life had been stolen. He stood there, surrounded by the ghosts of the past, trying to make sense of the senseless. He realized that he would never fully understand the darkness that had consumed David, but he could find solace in knowing that justice had been served.

He visited Sarah's grave, the weathered headstone bearing her name etched in the stone. He laid a single white rose, a token of his love and grief. As he stood there, the setting sun casting long shadows across the cemetery, he felt a wave of emotions wash over him: grief, anger, acceptance.

He knew that Sarah's memory would forever be a part of him, a constant reminder of the fragility of life and the enduring power of love. The investigation had left scars, both physical and emotional, but it had also brought him a sense of purpose, a renewed determination to fight for justice and to protect those he loved.

As he drove away, the fading light casting a warm glow across the landscape, he realized that his journey was far from over. There were still unanswered questions, lingering doubts that wouldn't be silenced. But he knew that he would continue to search for the truth, to honor Sarah's memory and to fight for a world where justice prevailed.

John's investigation led him to the doorstep of a local photography studio, nestled in a quaint corner of the city. The studio, with its faded sign and worn-out window displays, seemed to whisper stories of bygone eras. He was greeted by a woman with weary eyes and a gentle smile, her name, Mrs. Amelia, etched in the faded lettering above the counter.

"David," she said, her voice a soft murmur, "He used to work here. He was a talented photographer, at least that's what we thought." She sighed, her gaze flickering towards the dusty shelves lined with albums and framed prints. "He had this... intensity about him. I always felt a little uneasy around him."

Amelia recounted David's sudden disappearance, the rumors that swirled around him, and the unsettling aura that lingered in the studio after his departure. "He was let go," she confided, her voice dropping to a hushed whisper. "There were complaints. Harassment, you see. Unwanted attention. He had a way of making people feel uncomfortable, like he was always watching them."

Amelia's words sent a shiver down John's spine. The pieces were starting to fall into place, forming a chilling picture. He had been right to trust his gut instinct; the man in the photograph, the one who had been with Sarah, was no ordinary passerby. He was a predator, a man with a troubled past and a history of inappropriate behavior.

With a renewed sense of urgency, John delved deeper

into David's history. He sought information from the local police department, uncovering reports of domestic violence and a string of misdemeanor offenses related to stalking. His heart sank with each new detail, realizing the extent of David's dangerous nature.

But the investigation didn't stop there. John had a hunch that David's connection to Sarah went beyond a mere chance encounter. He needed more. He needed to understand what David had been doing with Sarah, what had drawn him to her. He needed to see the truth behind the lens of David's camera.

He revisited the studio, this time seeking not Amelia's memories, but the remnants of David's work. Amelia, a bit hesitant at first, reluctantly agreed to show him David's collection of negatives, stored in a dusty box tucked away in the back room. She warned him, her voice laced with concern, "He used to take pictures of everyone, even without asking. He had a fascination with capturing people's moments, their secrets."

John spent hours examining the negatives, his fingers tracing the delicate contours of the images. Most were ordinary snapshots - couples laughing at a picnic, children playing in a park, mundane glimpses of everyday life. But then, he found them. The photographs of Sarah.

The first photograph was a candid shot of Sarah walking down a bustling city street, her face turned away from the camera. Her hair, cascading over her shoulders, seemed to shimmer in the afternoon sun. Her figure, slender and graceful, was almost ethereal.

The next photograph was more disturbing. It showed Sarah sitting in a cafe, lost in a book, her face shrouded in shadow. But there, in the background, was David, his face obscured by the low light, a shadowy figure observing Sarah from a distance.

The photographs became increasingly unsettling, each one depicting Sarah unaware, a constant presence of David lurking in the background, his lens trained on her every move. The chilling nature of these photographs, the way they captured Sarah's unawareness, the obsession that David harbored in his heart, sent a chill down John's spine.

These were not innocent snapshots. These were fragments of a twisted obsession, a slow and insidious descent into the abyss of stalking. They were glimpses into the dark mind of a man who had preyed on Sarah, his camera an extension of his possessive desires.

John knew that these photographs held the key to understanding David's motive, his connection to Sarah, the reason he had been with her on that fateful day. He had to decipher the narrative that unfolded in these images, to piece together the story of Sarah's last moments, to unravel the secrets that David had captured behind his lens.

Armed with these photographs, John felt a surge of renewed purpose. He had finally found a tangible link, a concrete clue that would lead him to the truth. The killer's identity was slowly coming into focus. He was not a mere stranger, a phantom from Sarah's past. He was a man with a face, a name, a history, and a chillingly familiar obsession with capturing the moments of his victim. John knew that with these photographs, he was one step closer to solving the mystery that had haunted him for years.

John, fueled by a mix of determination and despair, tracked down the owner of the "Shutter & Light" photography studio, a weathered man named Arthur with eyes that held the wisdom of countless captured moments. Arthur, initially hesitant, agreed to talk, his voice raspy with age. He confirmed David's employment, a young man with an uncanny talent for capturing fleeting expressions and raw emotions. However, his passion was often overshadowed by a disturbing obsession.

"He wasn't just good, John, he was brilliant," Arthur sighed, leaning back in his worn leather chair, "but he had this... darkness. It started subtly, an unnerving intensity in his gaze when he worked with certain subjects, particularly women."

John pressed, his intuition tingling. "Did he ever work with my sister, Sarah?"

Arthur's brow furrowed, a flicker of recognition in his eyes. "Sarah... yes, she came in for a portrait session about a year before she... disappeared. It was strange, he seemed... fixated on her, even after the session ended."

He retrieved a dusty, leather-bound album from a shelf, the cover adorned with a faded inscription: "Shutter & Light: 1998." With trembling hands, he turned to a specific page, revealing a series of photographs, each one capturing Sarah in various poses, seemingly unaware of the camera's presence.

John's stomach churned. The photographs, taken in a candid style, showed Sarah walking down a bustling street, her laughter echoing in the air, her eyes sparkling with life. But as he flipped through the pages, a chilling pattern emerged.

David had followed Sarah, his camera capturing her moments of vulnerability, of solitude, of carefree joy. In one photo, Sarah was sitting on a park bench, her head bowed as she read a book, her face bathed in a soft, golden light. In another, she was walking into a bookstore, her back turned to the camera, her silhouette framed by a doorway.

The photographs felt intrusive, an invasion of privacy. John felt a surge of rage and protectiveness for his sister, realizing that David had been stalking her, documenting her every move, without her knowledge.

"He wasn't supposed to take those," Arthur said, his voice choked with emotion. "I told him to stop, but he wouldn't listen. He said he was inspired by her beauty, by her... energy."

John felt a wave of nausea, a sense of violation. "Where did he take these pictures?"

Arthur hesitated, his gaze avoiding John's. "He didn't tell me. He said he needed to keep them for his... inspiration."

The truth was dawning upon John. The killer was David, and the photographs were not just a creepy obsession, they were a perverse chronicle of his stalking, a prelude to his crime.

"Did you ever think he might be dangerous, Arthur?" John asked, his voice barely a whisper.

Arthur shook his head, his face etched with regret. "I didn't know. I didn't want to believe it. But now... seeing these, seeing the way he looked at her, it all makes sense."

John felt a surge of adrenaline, his mind racing with possibilities. He needed to find the location where David had taken these pictures, to search for any other clues that might help him piece together the events leading to Sarah's disappearance. He had to find Sarah, and he had to bring David to justice.

John left Arthur's studio, the weight of the photographs pressing down on his shoulders. His mind was flooded with images of Sarah, a vision of her carefree smile and sparkling eyes, now tragically tainted by the knowledge of David's chilling obsession.

He reached for his phone, dialing the number of a trusted forensic expert, a woman named Dr. Emily Carter. He needed her help to analyze the photographs, to find any trace of evidence, any hint of a location, any detail that might lead him to the truth.

"Emily, I need your expertise," he said, his voice strained with urgency. "I found something that might be crucial to the case. I think I might know who the killer is."

Emily's voice was calm, reassuring, "Tell me everything, John. We need to look at everything with fresh eyes."

John shared his findings, the chilling photographs and the haunting pattern they revealed. He spoke of David's unsettling obsession, his clandestine photography sessions, the eerie sense of violation. He poured out his frustration, his fear, his desperate need for answers.

"I think I need to see these photographs, John," Emily said, her voice firm but kind. "They might hold the key to unlocking this mystery."

John arranged to meet Emily at her lab the following morning, the photographs tucked securely in his jacket pocket. He knew he had to find Sarah, to bring her home. He owed her that, and he owed her killer a reckoning.

The weight of the photographs was a constant reminder of Sarah's vulnerability, of David's chilling obsession, and of the long, difficult road ahead. John knew he was entering a dangerous game, a game of shadows and secrets, where the stakes were higher than ever before. But he was determined to win, to unravel the truth and bring justice to his sister's memory.

John's heart pounded in his chest as he stared at the photographs David had taken of Sarah. Each image was a chilling reminder of David's obsession and the sinister way he had preyed upon his sister. The photos revealed a series of interactions between David and Sarah, capturing glimpses of her last moments, her unsuspecting smile, and the growing fear in her eyes. The photographs were a silent testament to the terror that had consumed Sarah in her final days.

John studied the locations in each photo, hoping to piece together the timeline of Sarah's final moments. The photographs revealed a pattern, a meticulous and insidious stalking that David had carefully orchestrated. The locations, seemingly random at first, began to form a chilling narrative.

John carefully scrutinized the details in the background of the photos, seeking any clues that could help him pinpoint the location where David had last taken Sarah. He noticed a distinctive pattern of brickwork, a unique architectural element that he recognized from his childhood. It was the same brick pattern he had seen on the back wall of the old bakery, a place that had been abandoned for years.

The bakery was a place where Sarah and her friends often gathered for late-night talks and laughter. John remembered the bakery vividly, the scent of fresh bread and the warmth of the oven. But he had never thought that this place would become the stage for his sister's final moments.

John's mind raced with a growing sense of dread as he remembered the eyewitness account. The witness had described the man who had been with Sarah as having a tattoo on his wrist, a tattoo that perfectly matched the one David had. And the witness had mentioned a specific location – a place where Sarah had gone with the man. John's heart sank as he realized that the location matched the description of the bakery.

The realization hit John like a physical blow. It was the bakery. The place where Sarah had shared countless happy memories had become the scene of her last moments. The photographs provided a crucial connection, linking David to the bakery and placing him at the heart of the mystery.

John's determination solidified. He had to confront David, to unravel the truth behind his obsession with Sarah and the terrifying events that had led to her disappearance. John was fueled by a burning desire for justice, a need to bring his sister's killer to account and to find solace in the revelation of the truth.

He reached for his phone, his fingers trembling slightly as he dialed the number of the local police department. He needed to act quickly, to secure the location and to gather the necessary evidence to prove David's guilt. As he spoke to the officer on the other end of the line, his mind raced with a mixture of fear and determination. He had finally found the key to unlocking the mystery of his sister's disappearance.

The next few hours were a blur of activity. John, driven by his relentless pursuit of the truth, coordinated with the police to secure the bakery. He worked tirelessly with the forensic team, meticulously documenting every detail of the scene. The photographs provided a roadmap, guiding the investigation and revealing David's carefully crafted narrative.

The bakery was a silent testament to the tragic events that had unfolded within its walls. Every corner held a chilling reminder of Sarah's final moments, every crumb a fragment of her lost life. As John examined the scene, he couldn't help but feel a profound sense of grief for his sister, a wave of sorrow that washed over him like a tidal wave.

The investigation uncovered a chilling pattern of obsession, manipulation, and violence. David had meticulously stalked Sarah, carefully planning each encounter, each interaction, each step towards his sinister goal. He had captured her on camera, each image a snapshot of her growing fear, her desperate attempts to escape his relentless pursuit.

John was determined to find the final piece of the puzzle, the missing link that would confirm his suspicions and expose the truth. He examined the photographs again, searching for any clues that could reveal the truth about Sarah's final moments. He had to find the evidence that would prove David's guilt and bring justice to his sister's memory.

John's investigation was a journey through the darkest recesses of the human psyche. He had delved into the mind of a predator, a man consumed by a twisted obsession. He had faced the reality of his sister's tragic fate and the unsettling truth that her killer had been living among them, seemingly ordinary, seemingly harmless.

He searched through David's belongings, a meticulous and painstaking process that revealed a chilling portrait of a man consumed by a relentless obsession. He found notebooks filled with obsessive entries about Sarah, each page a testament to his unhealthy fixation. He discovered a collection of Sarah's personal items, carefully collected over time, a collection of stolen pieces of her life, a tangible reminder of his sinister intent.

The evidence was mounting, a tapestry of clues that pointed to David's guilt. He had finally found the answers he had been searching for for so many years. The weight of the truth pressed down on John, a crushing burden of realization that his sister's killer had been lurking in the shadows for so long.

The air hung heavy with unspoken tension as John sat across from David, the evidence laid out before them like a morbid tableau. It was a small, cramped room in the police station, devoid of the sterile, clinical feel of the interrogation room. The table between them was a makeshift altar of truth, adorned with photographs, documents, and a single, haunting vintage camera.

John had finally tracked down David, the photographer with the haunting connection to Sarah's disappearance. Each piece of evidence, meticulously collected over months of relentless investigation, whispered the truth: David had been obsessed with Sarah, his fascination morphing into something darker, something more sinister.

The photographs were the most damning evidence. Taken secretly, they captured Sarah in unguarded moments, her innocence oblivious to the unseen predator behind the lens. David's eyes, as captured by the camera's cold, unblinking gaze, held a chilling intensity, a possessive hunger that sent shivers down John's spine.

There was a photograph of Sarah at a coffee shop, a fleeting smile on her face as she read a book. In another, she was walking down a street, her silhouette framed against the setting sun. Every image was a testament to David's relentless pursuit, a chilling chronicle of his obsession.

John placed a photograph on the table, one that had been taken in a secluded park, the same park where Sarah's skeleton had been found. The camera angle was unusual, almost voyeuristic, capturing Sarah from a distance, her back to the camera. The picture was taken on the day Sarah vanished, a chilling detail that sent a jolt of icy dread through John.

"You stalked her, didn't you?" John's voice was low, laced with a suppressed fury that he could barely contain. "You followed her, watched her, took pictures of her without her knowing."

David's gaze was downcast, his shoulders slumped as if weighed down by the weight of his guilt. His hands, once steady and confident, now trembled slightly, his fingers nervously tracing the worn surface of the table. The silence stretched out between them, heavy and suffocating, a testament to the unspoken truth that hung in the air.

"I...I couldn't help myself," David finally mumbled, his voice barely audible. "I was drawn to her, obsessed with her."

"Drawn to her? You followed her, took pictures of her in secret, and then...you took her life." John's voice was a sharp edge, cutting through the thick silence. "This wasn't obsession, David. This was something far darker, something far more sinister."

David looked up, his eyes filled with a mixture of fear and despair. His expression was that of a trapped animal, caught in the unforgiving light of truth. He opened his mouth to speak, but no words came out. The shame was etched on his face, his lips trembling as if a silent scream was locked behind them.

"Don't you dare try to explain it," John snapped, his voice laced with an unforgiving rage. "You don't get to explain away murder, David. You don't get to justify your actions. You took Sarah's life, and nothing you say can ever change that."

A single tear rolled down David's cheek, a silent testament to his shame. He looked at the photographs on the table, each one a reflection of his twisted obsession, each one a frozen moment in time that captured his descent into darkness.

"I...I didn't mean to hurt her," David stammered, his voice thick with emotion. "It just...happened. I was so caught up in my obsession, I...I lost control."

"Lost control?" John scoffed. "You call that losing control? You followed her, took pictures of her, and then you killed her. You planned it, David. You thought about it. You executed it. And now, you're trying to tell me that it was just a mistake, a slip-up, a moment of madness?"

David's face crumpled, his shoulders sagging even further. His body seemed to shrink, as if the weight of his guilt was pulling him down, down into the abyss of his own darkness.

"I was...I was afraid," David whispered, his voice barely a breath. "I was afraid of losing her, of her getting away from me. I...I wanted her to be mine, forever."

John felt a pang of pity for David, a fleeting moment of

understanding for the man who had been consumed by a dark obsession. But the pity was fleeting, quickly replaced by a simmering rage that fueled his relentless pursuit of justice for Sarah.

"Forever?" John echoed, his voice laced with sarcasm. "You took her life, David. You robbed her of her future, of her dreams, of her love, of her life. Forever? What kind of forever is that, David? What kind of love is that?"

David's eyes welled up with tears. He reached for a tissue, his hand shaking as he fumbled with the box. His face was a mask of despair, his soul a mirror reflecting the darkness he had allowed to consume him.

"I'm…I'm sorry," David choked out, his voice barely audible. "I'm so sorry. I know I can't take it back, but I'm so sorry."

The words hung in the air, heavy and hollow. John looked at David, his eyes searching for any sign of remorse, any glimmer of genuine regret. But all he saw was the reflection of a broken man, consumed by his own darkness.

John rose from his chair, his movements stiff and deliberate. He stood over David, his gaze piercing the man's soul. He was no longer a detective, no longer a brother seeking justice for his sister. He was a man filled with rage, his heart a furnace fueled by the pain of loss, the torment of Sarah's absence.

"Sorry?" John spat, his voice dripping with venom. "Sorry doesn't bring her back, David. Sorry doesn't undo what you did. Sorry doesn't erase the pain you caused."

John turned away, his anger a storm brewing within him. He had found the killer, the man who had taken Sarah's life and left a gaping hole in their family's heart. But the truth had brought no solace, no healing. It had only confirmed the painful reality of Sarah's absence and the chilling knowledge that her killer had been hiding in plain sight.

As John walked out of the room, the image of David's crumpled form haunted him. The confession, the truth, had brought a sense of closure, but it had also left a gaping wound, a void that no amount of justice could ever fill.

Chapter 4: The Weight of Truth

The weight of the investigation settled on John like a suffocating blanket. He'd finally caught the man who had taken Sarah from them, the man who had lived among them for years, hiding his dark secret. Justice had been served, but the victory felt hollow.

John's world was a whirlwind of emotions—relief, a sense of closure, but also a crushing weight of grief that refused to lift. He'd known the investigation would be tough, that he'd have to confront demons he'd buried for years, but he hadn't anticipated the gut-wrenching realization that the man who had ended Sarah's life had been someone they'd considered a friend, a familiar face.

The news had hit his family like a tidal wave. His parents, aged and frail, were shattered. The news had ripped open old wounds, forcing them to relive the agonizing day Sarah disappeared. They struggled to reconcile the image of David, the friendly face who'd often helped around the house, with the monster who had taken their daughter.

John, too, was grappling with the enormity of what he'd uncovered. The case had been more than just an investigation; it had been a personal journey, a painful exploration of his own grief and guilt. He couldn't shake the feeling that he'd failed Sarah, that he hadn't been there to protect her.

The investigation had left indelible marks on John's soul.

He'd been forced to confront the darkest corners of human nature, the capacity for evil that lurked beneath the surface of seemingly ordinary people. He'd seen the fragility of trust, the ease with which deception could be woven into the fabric of everyday life.

The weight of Sarah's death, of the years he'd spent searching for her, of the revelation that her killer had been a familiar face, pressed down on him relentlessly. It was a burden he carried with him constantly, a reminder of his own mortality and the fleeting nature of life.

John found solace in knowing that he had brought Sarah's killer to justice, but it wasn't enough to ease the pain. He missed her deeply, the laughter she'd brought into their lives, her infectious spirit. He missed the conversations, the shared memories, the simple act of her presence. He missed her terribly.

He visited Sarah's grave, a simple headstone in a quiet corner of the cemetery. He sat there for hours, surrounded by the silence of the dead, sharing his memories with her. He spoke of her laughter, her dreams, the way she'd always had a mischievous glint in her eyes.

He apologized for not being able to bring her back, for not being able to protect her. He told her that he loved her, that he would never forget her. He vowed to live his life in a way that would honor her memory, to fight for justice and truth, to never forget the importance of family and love.

He left Sarah's grave with a heavy heart but with a sliver of peace. He'd finally found some closure, a way to acknowledge her death and to begin the process of moving forward. He knew the pain of her loss would always be with him, but he also knew that he had to find a way to live with it, to honor her memory by living a life filled with purpose and meaning.

The investigation had left him changed, scarred by the darkness he'd encountered, but also strengthened by the experience. He was no longer the same John Snider, the carefree detective who'd once believed in the good in people. He'd seen too much darkness, too much evil to maintain that naivety. But he wasn't broken either. He was stronger, more determined, more aware of the complexities of human nature, the fragility of life, and the importance of fighting for justice.

The weight of the investigation would always be with him, a reminder of the darkness that lurked beneath the surface of the world, but it would also be a reminder of the strength he'd found within himself, of the love he had for his family, and of the enduring power of hope. John knew that he would never truly be free of the burden of Sarah's death, but he was determined to live a life worthy of her memory, to fight for justice and truth, and to never forget the importance of family and love.

The revelation of Sarah's fate shattered the fragile peace that had settled over the Snider family. The weight of the truth, like a heavy cloak, draped over them, suffocating their grief and replacing it with a stark, unforgiving reality. They had lost their beloved Sarah, their daughter, their sister, their friend, and the person responsible for her demise was none other than David, a man they had considered a friend, a trusted acquaintance.

John, burdened with the knowledge of his sister's fate, felt a profound sense of betrayal. The man he had once shared meals with, the one who had offered condolences during those agonizing years of searching, had been the architect of Sarah's demise. The realization was a blow, a gut-wrenching revelation that tore at the very fabric of his trust.

He looked at his parents, their faces etched with a mixture of sorrow and disbelief. Their eyes held the flicker of a thousand unanswered questions, the pain of a truth that had been hidden for years, now laid bare before them. Their trust had been violated, their love for Sarah tainted by the dark reality of her murder.

"How could we have been so blind?" his mother whispered, her voice trembling with a mixture of grief and anger. "How could we have missed all the signs?"

John, unable to offer solace, simply nodded, his own heart echoing the same question. They had been so focused on the possibility of an outsider, a stranger lurking in the shadows, that they had overlooked the truth that lay hidden in plain sight.

The revelation of David's actions sent shockwaves through the family. Their memories of him, once tinged with warmth and affection, were now overshadowed by the chilling reality of his crimes. The weight of guilt and shame pressed down on them, leaving a sense of unease that lingered in every corner of their home.

John's younger brother, Mark, initially struggled to comprehend the depth of the tragedy. He was too young to remember Sarah's disappearance, but the weight of the truth began to manifest in his childish nightmares and a sudden, unexplained fear of the dark.

Mark, in his innocence, had always considered David a friendly presence, a source of comfort and amusement. Now, he was forced to confront the fact that the man who had once entertained him with silly stories had been responsible for taking away his sister, a sister he had never truly known.

The Snider family was torn apart by the realization that their world had been built on a foundation of deceit. The man they had trusted, the man who had appeared in their lives like a comforting beacon of normalcy, had been a wolf in sheep's clothing, a predator who had preyed on their loved one.

The weight of their collective grief was compounded by the knowledge that they had been living a lie, a life built on a foundation of misplaced trust. John knew that the healing process would be long and arduous, a journey of confronting their pain and learning to live with the enduring scar of Sarah's absence.

The family was left with a profound sense of loss, a void that could never be filled. Their home, once filled with laughter and the echoes of Sarah's vibrant spirit, now carried the silent weight of her absence. Their lives had been forever altered, the remnants of their former selves shattered by the truth that had finally come to light.

John, determined to honor his sister's memory, vowed to find a way to move forward, to find a path to healing and reconciliation. He knew that the road ahead would be fraught with challenges, but he was resolute in his commitment to finding peace amidst the wreckage of their shattered lives. He knew that Sarah's spirit would guide him, her memory a beacon of light in the darkness that had enveloped their world.

The Snider family, though broken, clung to each other, finding strength in their shared grief and a glimmer of hope in the prospect of healing. They knew that the road ahead would be difficult, but they were determined to find a way to navigate the treacherous waters of their loss and emerge, one day, into the light of acceptance and peace. They would honor Sarah's memory by living lives filled with love, compassion, and the enduring power of forgiveness.

The investigation had carved a chasm within John, a wound that refused to heal. It had been a relentless pursuit, a desperate attempt to bring his sister back from the abyss, but all he had found were the echoes of her absence. The weight of the revelation – that Sarah's killer had lived among them, a familiar face hidden in the shadows – had settled in his soul, a heavy cloak of grief and despair.

John saw the world differently now. He had always believed in the power of truth, in the resilience of justice, but the chilling reality of his sister's fate had shattered that belief. It had been a devastating discovery, the realization that the people he knew, the people he trusted, were capable of unimaginable acts. The killer had been a shadow in the corner of his vision, a haunting presence in his family's life, and now, John was left to grapple with the agonizing truth.

He had spent years trying to forget, to bury the pain of Sarah's disappearance, but now it had resurfaced, amplified by the revelation of her killer's identity. The past, like a persistent ghost, refused to be silenced. It clung to him, a constant reminder of what had been lost. He could see the shadows of his sister's laughter in the familiar corners of his home, hear the whispers of her voice in the rustling of leaves, feel the ghost of her touch in the warmth of the sun on his skin.

John found solace in the knowledge that justice had been served, that Sarah's killer would face the consequences of his actions. Yet, the ache of her absence remained, a hollow space in his heart that could never be filled. He knew that the past could never truly be forgotten, that the scars it left would remain, a constant reminder of the fragility of life and the fleeting nature of happiness.

He realized that he carried the weight of his sister's fate

on his shoulders, a responsibility to honor her memory and to fight for a world where such tragedies were less likely to occur. The investigation had changed him, stripping away the naivety of his youth and replacing it with a hardened resolve. He was now a man of the world, his eyes opened to the darkness that lurked beneath the surface.

His family too, bore the weight of this truth. The revelation of Sarah's fate had fractured their world, casting a dark cloud over their lives. They were left to grapple with the pain of loss and the betrayal of trust. They had lost Sarah, and now, they were forced to confront the reality that the man they had once known was capable of such heinous acts.

John understood the complex tapestry of human emotions, the intricate interplay of love, loss, and betrayal. He saw the pain in his family's eyes, the struggle to reconcile the man they knew with the monster he had become. He knew that their journey to healing would be long and arduous, but he hoped that they could find a way to find solace in each other's embrace, a way to rebuild their lives from the ruins of the past.

The investigation had left John with a sense of bittersweet closure. The truth, as he had found it, was a double-edged sword, offering justice but also leaving behind a trail of broken hearts and shattered dreams. He understood that the past could never be erased, that its scars would forever remain, a testament to the fragility of life and the enduring power of love.

But John had also found a new strength, a renewed purpose. He had faced his fears, confronted the darkness, and emerged with a deeper understanding of the world and the people in it. He knew that he could never truly forget, but he could choose to move forward, to find meaning and purpose in the face of loss. He carried the memory of Sarah with him, a constant reminder of the love that bound them, a promise to honor her life and to strive for a world where such tragedies would be less likely to occur.

The cemetery was silent, save for the gentle rustling of leaves in the autumn breeze. John stood before Sarah's headstone, the inscription etched in the cold, gray stone a constant reminder of her absence. He ran a hand along the smooth surface, the coolness seeping into his skin, grounding him in the reality of her death. He hadn't been here in years. The weight of his sister's unsolved disappearance had been a burden he carried with him, a heavy cloak draped across his shoulders. He hadn't been able to face this place, this final resting place for his sister, until now.

The weight of the past was finally lifting, though the pain still lingered. The investigation had been brutal, a relentless pursuit of justice that had chipped away at his soul. The revelation of David's confession, the chilling reality of his obsession with Sarah, had been a punch to the gut, leaving him reeling with shock and disbelief. Yet, there was a sense of closure, a sliver of peace he hadn't felt in years. The truth had been exposed, a venomous serpent finally revealed, leaving John gasping for air after years of suffocating silence.

John pulled out the vintage camera, the one that had held the blurry photo, the single piece of evidence that had led him to David. He held it close, the cool metal against his cheek, as he reminisced. The camera had been a portal, a window into Sarah's final moments, revealing the sinister truth lurking beneath the surface of their small town. He looked at the photo again, the blurred image of his sister, her face a ghost in the fading light. He could almost see her smile, hear her laugh, feel the warmth of her presence. A wave of grief washed over him, leaving him breathless.

"I miss you, Sarah," he whispered, his voice hoarse. He spoke of the memories he held close, the silly childhood games they played, the secrets they shared, the dreams they had. He spoke of the pain of her absence, the emptiness that had settled in his heart, a void that could never be filled. He spoke of the guilt he had carried, the belief that he could have done more, could have protected her, could have kept her safe.

John spoke of the investigation, of the arduous journey, the agonizing twists and turns, the relentless pursuit of the truth. He spoke of the sleepless nights, the endless hours spent poring over evidence, the constant pressure to find answers, to bring Sarah's killer to justice. He spoke of the emotional toll the case had taken, the fear, the anger, the despair. But he also spoke of the hope, the unwavering determination that had fueled his pursuit. He spoke of the need to find closure, to honor his sister's memory by revealing the truth, by ensuring that her killer would face the consequences of his actions.

John spoke of the family, of the pain they shared, the grief that bound them together, the struggle to come to terms with Sarah's death. He spoke of the questions they still carried, the lingering doubts and uncertainties. He spoke of the strength they found in their shared sorrow, the love that had weathered the storm.

As the sun began to set, casting long shadows across the cemetery, John felt a sense of peace wash over him. He had come here to find closure, to release the burden of his sister's unsolved disappearance, and he felt he had. The truth, though painful, had set him free. Sarah's killer had been brought to justice, and the weight of his sister's case no longer crushed him.

He stood for a moment longer, his gaze fixed on the headstone, before turning to leave. He knew he would never truly forget, that the pain of his sister's loss would always be a part of him. But he also knew that he would carry her memory with him, a reminder of the love they shared, the lessons he had learned, and the strength he had found. He would honor her memory by living a life filled with love, compassion, and justice, a life worthy of the sister he loved.

The weight of the investigation hung heavy on John's shoulders. He had found his sister's killer, had brought him to justice, but the feeling of closure he had hoped for was elusive. The years of searching, the agonizing uncertainty, the torment of wondering what had happened to Sarah, had left an indelible mark on him.

He carried the memory of Sarah with him, the image of her bright smile and infectious laugh forever etched in his heart. But now, those memories were intertwined with the chilling reality of her death, the knowledge that she had been taken from them by a man who had lived among them, a man they had trusted.

The revelation that David, the seemingly harmless employee, had been responsible for Sarah's disappearance had shattered his world. It had left him questioning everything he had thought he knew about people, about the world around him.

He had caught David in a web of lies and deceit, his confession revealing a twisted obsession with Sarah that had escalated into a horrifying act of violence. But even as he listened to David's confession, a sliver of doubt lingered in John's mind. He couldn't shake the feeling that there was something missing, that there were other forces at play. The investigation had been a long and arduous journey, filled with twists and turns, dead ends, and unexpected revelations.

Each clue, each discovery, had brought him closer to the truth, but it had also peeled back layers of his own life, exposing the cracks in his carefully constructed world. He had delved into his family's past, unearthing secrets and resentments that had been buried for years.

He had confronted the ghosts of his own childhood, facing the painful memories of his sister's disappearance and the lingering guilt he felt for not being able to protect her. The weight of the investigation, the burden of his sister's death, and the emotional toll of confronting the darkness within himself had left John weary, but also strangely, more alive than he had ever felt.

He had faced his own mortality, confronted the fragility of life, and found a renewed appreciation for the people he loved and the precious moments they shared. He had learned the value of forgiveness, not just for his sister's killer, but also for himself. He had learned to forgive himself for the things he hadn't done, for the choices he had made, and for the burden he had carried for so long.

The investigation had not brought him the closure he had hoped for, but it had given him a different kind of peace. It had given him a sense of purpose, a renewed drive to find justice for those who had been wronged.

He had found solace in the support of his family and friends, in the love and compassion that surrounded him. He had discovered a strength he didn't know he possessed, a resilience that had been forged in the crucible of his grief.

He knew that the scars of the past would never fully fade, that the memory of Sarah would forever be a part of him. But he also knew that he would carry her memory with him as a source of strength, a reminder of the importance of love, family, and the enduring power of hope.

The weight of the investigation, the emotional journey he had taken, had changed John in profound ways. He had learned to face his own vulnerabilities, to confront the darkness within himself, and to find the courage to seek truth and justice, even in the face of overwhelming pain and loss.

The world around him seemed brighter, more alive, as if he had been reborn through his experience. The investigation had been a painful ordeal, but it had also been a journey of self-discovery, a path to healing, and a testament to the enduring power of the human spirit.

He still looked at the vintage camera, the one that held the blurry photograph of Sarah's final moments, with a mixture of sadness and gratitude. The camera was a symbol of the truth that had been hidden for so long, a reminder of the importance of persistence and the power of a single image to reveal a hidden truth.

The camera was also a reminder of the lasting impact of his sister's disappearance, of the profound ways it had changed him and the world around him. He held the camera close, feeling its weight in his hands, and he whispered a silent prayer for Sarah, for her peace, and for his own.

As he walked away, he looked back at the grave, the gentle breeze rustling the leaves of the weeping willow that stood guard over it. The world was a different place now, a world that had been forever altered by the events of the investigation.

He knew that the past could never be erased, that the

memories of his sister would forever be a part of him. But he also knew that he would carry those memories with him, not as a source of pain, but as a source of strength, a reminder of the love and compassion that had sustained him through his darkest hours.

John was left with a bittersweet sense of closure. He had found justice for his sister, but he had also found a new understanding of himself, of the world around him, and of the enduring power of hope. The case had left a profound impact on his life, shaping his view of the world and the importance of family and forgiveness.

The memories of Sarah, the love and laughter they had shared, would forever be a part of him, a reminder that even in the face of tragedy, life can find a way to bloom anew. He knew that his journey was not over, that there were still challenges ahead. But he also knew that he was not alone, that he had the strength and resilience to face whatever life threw his way. He would continue to honor Sarah's memory by striving for justice and seeking truth in all that he did. He would never forget her, and he would never give up on finding a sense of peace and closure.

Chapter 8: The Skeleton's Lens

The vintage camera, now resting in a glass case on his desk, had become a symbol of truth, a stark reminder of the secrets buried deep within the earth. John ran his fingers along its worn leather casing, the coolness of the metal sending a shiver down his spine. The camera had held the key to Sarah's disappearance, a single, blurry photograph that had opened the door to a truth hidden for decades.

He remembered the day he received the call, a whisper of hope amidst the crushing weight of years of unanswered questions. The discovery of the skeleton, a chilling reminder of Sarah's fate, had been accompanied by the camera, an unexpected artifact that held the potential to break the silence.

The photograph, though blurry, had captured a fleeting moment, a glimpse of a shadowed figure lurking behind Sarah, a figure that John had recognized as David, a man he had once considered a friend. That blurry image had become the lens through which John had peered into the depths of his sister's past, a past filled with secrets and lies, a past that had finally yielded its truth.

The camera, he realized, was more than just a tool; it was a testament to the power of a single image, a snapshot frozen in time, a moment that had held the key to unlocking a long-forgotten truth. It was a symbol of persistence, a reminder that even in the face of uncertainty and pain, the pursuit of truth was paramount.

As he looked at the camera, John couldn't help but feel a sense of gratitude for the investigators who had uncovered the truth. They had meticulously examined the photograph, painstakingly piecing together the fragments of Sarah's final moments. They had followed every lead, every whisper of information, until they had finally arrived at the truth, bringing an end to the long-standing mystery that had haunted him for so many years.

The camera, he realized, also represented the importance of forgiveness. John had spent years consumed by anger and resentment, a constant ache in his heart that had refused to subside. But as he finally came to terms with Sarah's fate, he also realized that the path to healing lay in forgiveness.

He couldn't condone David's actions, the horrific crime he had committed. But he understood that holding onto the anger would only serve to poison his soul, keeping him trapped in a cycle of bitterness and pain. Forgiveness, he realized, was not about erasing the past or accepting the actions of the perpetrator. It was about releasing the burden of anger and resentment, allowing himself to finally move forward.

The camera also served as a constant reminder of the enduring power of love. Even though Sarah was gone, the love he had for her remained, a powerful force that had guided him through his darkest moments. The investigation, he realized, had not only brought him justice, but it had also strengthened the bonds of his family, reinforcing the importance of love and support during times of grief and despair.

As he held the camera, John felt a sense of peace settle over him, a feeling he had not experienced in years. The truth had been uncovered, justice had been served, and he had found forgiveness, not only for David, but for himself. He was finally free from the burden of his sister's unsolved disappearance, and the weight of the past had begun to lift.

The camera, however, remained a symbol of the past, a tangible reminder of the tragedy he had endured. It was a memento that he would keep close, a constant reminder of the importance of seeking truth, the power of forgiveness, and the enduring power of love. It was a lens through which he could look back at his sister's life, remembering her not as a victim, but as a woman who had lived a full and complex life, a life that had been tragically cut short.

The camera had become a symbol of his journey, a journey that had been filled with pain and loss, but also with hope and resilience. It was a testament to his determination to find the truth, to seek justice, and to find peace in the aftermath of his sister's disappearance. It was a reminder that even in the darkest of times, love and forgiveness could prevail, and that the human spirit could find a way to heal and move forward.

The blurry photo in the vintage camera became a symbol for me. It was a symbol of truth, the truth that had been hidden for so long. The camera held a single image, a fleeting moment captured in time, but that moment revealed everything. It revealed the killer, the secret, the truth.

Looking back, I see the power of that single image. It was like a small seed, planted in the fertile ground of my determination. That seed, nurtured by my unwavering resolve, blossomed into a full-fledged investigation, a relentless pursuit of truth. The camera, the photo, it became a symbol of the enduring power of truth. It reminded me that even in the face of uncertainty, even in the face of pain, truth has a way of emerging. It takes time, it takes effort, it takes a relentless commitment to uncovering the truth, but it will emerge.

As I contemplated the power of that single image, I also began to reflect on the power of forgiveness. Forgiveness wasn't easy. It wasn't about condoning the actions of the killer. It wasn't about forgetting the pain. It was about releasing myself from the burden of anger and hatred.

I realized that anger was a heavy cloak, weighing me down, suffocating me. It kept me tethered to the past, preventing me from moving forward. I was trapped in a cycle of anger, consumed by the pain of my sister's death, and it only served to fuel my own suffering. Forgiveness, I realized, was the key to breaking free.

Forgiving the killer didn't mean forgetting Sarah. It didn't diminish her memory. It didn't make her death any less tragic. Forgiveness was about recognizing that the killer was also a victim, a victim of his own demons, his own twisted desires. It was about recognizing that his actions were a reflection of his own pain, his own brokenness.

Forgiving him, I realized, was a gift to myself. It was a way to finally release myself from the chains of anger and hatred that had been binding me for so long. It was a way to find peace, a way to move forward. It was a way to finally embrace the future, a future that I had been too afraid to face.

The road to forgiveness was a long and winding one. It was a journey filled with obstacles and detours. It was a journey that required courage, compassion, and a willingness to let go. It was a journey that challenged my deepest beliefs and forced me to confront my own demons.

As I struggled with the concept of forgiveness, I found solace in the support of my family and friends. Their love and compassion helped me through the darkest of times. They reminded me that I was not alone and that I had the strength to find my way back to the light.

They, too, had been victims of the killer's actions. They had lost Sarah, their beloved daughter and sister, and they had suffered deeply as a result. Yet, despite their own pain, they were able to offer me support and guidance. Their love, their understanding, their

unwavering belief in me, helped me to find the courage to forgive.

Forgiveness was a gift I gave to myself, but it was also a gift I gave to Sarah. It was a way to honor her memory, to ensure that her death wouldn't define my life. It was a way to ensure that her legacy would be one of love, compassion, and hope.

Forgiveness was the key to my own healing. It was the key to finally breaking free from the chains of anger and hatred. It was the key to finding peace and moving forward. It was the key to finally embracing the future, a future that was filled with hope and possibility.

It took time, it took effort, it took a willingness to let go, but I found forgiveness. And in finding forgiveness, I found myself.

The weight of the investigation pressed down on John, a heavy cloak of grief and exhaustion. He had found his sister's killer, but the revelation had brought no sense of closure, only a hollow ache that resonated in the empty space she had left behind. His family, like a ship weathering a storm, struggled to stay afloat in the tumultuous wake of the revelation. The image of Sarah, vibrant and full of life, was now permanently intertwined with the cold, brutal reality of her disappearance.

His parents, their faces etched with a lifetime of unspoken pain, were left to grapple with the unbearable truth that their daughter's life had been stolen. Their

grief, a silent, simmering volcano, threatened to erupt at any moment. John, their anchor in the storm, held them close, offering the only solace he could – the strength of his presence and the unwavering certainty that Sarah would not be forgotten.

He had spent years carrying the burden of Sarah's unsolved case, a heavy stone in his chest, a constant reminder of his failure to protect her. But the weight of her disappearance had shifted, replaced by the crushing realization that her killer had lived amongst them, a wolf in sheep's clothing. The trust that had once been a cornerstone of their family life was now a fragile, shattered relic.

As he sat with his family, each face a canvas of sorrow, John felt an overwhelming sense of responsibility. He had sought justice for Sarah, but the scars of her disappearance remained, a constant reminder of the fragility of life. He saw the pain in their eyes, the shadows that had settled around their once bright smiles. He felt a renewed determination, a fire ignited by the need to rebuild what had been broken, to find a way forward, together.

He understood that they were all navigating the treacherous waters of grief, each in their own way. His brother, Mike, a reserved man who rarely expressed his emotions, retreated into his own world, finding solace in the familiar routine of his life. John saw the pain etched in Mike's silence, the unspoken words that hung in the air between them.

He recognized the strength in Mike's silence, the way he carried his grief with a quiet dignity. It was a strength that John admired, a resilience he had always known his brother possessed. He made a silent promise to himself, a vow to be there for Mike, to offer him the support he needed, even if it was only a listening ear or a shared silence.

His sister, Emily, the youngest of the family, was a whirlwind of emotions, her grief a volatile mix of anger, sadness, and confusion. John watched as she grappled with the pain of losing her sister, her anger directed at the world, at the injustice of it all. He saw the flicker of fear in her eyes, the fear of the unknown, the fear of being alone.

He knew that Emily needed to express her anger, to let it out, to process the overwhelming emotions that threatened to consume her. He offered her a shoulder to cry on, a listening ear to hear her rage. He understood that her anger was a shield, a way to protect herself from the pain that threatened to break her. He offered her the space to grieve, the freedom to express her emotions without judgment.

He knew that healing would take time, that the scars of their loss would linger, but he was determined to help them navigate the journey, to be their anchor in the storm. He was a shield against the world, a protector against the pain, and he vowed to remain steadfast in his duty to his family, a testament to the unbreakable bonds that united them.

John realized that their shared grief had become a shared strength, a force that bound them together. He saw the love that shone in their eyes, a love that transcended the pain, the love that reminded him that they were not alone. He found solace in their shared grief, the recognition that they were all in this together, united by their shared loss and their unyielding love for Sarah.

He understood that healing was not about forgetting but about learning to live with the pain, to carry the memory of their sister with them, to cherish the moments they had shared and to celebrate her life. He vowed to honor Sarah's memory by living a life filled with purpose, by seeking justice for those who had been wronged, and by spreading the message of love and compassion that had always been her guiding light.

As the sun set, casting long shadows across the land, John stood beside his family, a silent promise etched in his heart. He knew that their journey was just beginning, a journey of healing, of remembrance, and of enduring love. He had found answers, but the questions continued to linger, reminding him that the past was not a closed book but a tapestry woven with threads of grief, resilience, and love. He knew that the shadows of their past would always be with them, but he also knew that the light of their love would continue to shine, a beacon of hope in the darkness.

The silence of the empty room pressed in on John, a weight that mirrored the heaviness in his chest. He sat there, staring at the vintage camera, the one that held

the blurry photo, the only tangible link to his sister's final moments. It had been a long and arduous journey, filled with twists and turns, dead ends, and false leads. The investigation had taken him to the darkest corners of his own past, forced him to confront his deepest fears, and revealed the chilling truth that his sister's killer had been lurking in the shadows for decades.

The weight of the past, the burden of Sarah's disappearance, had consumed him for years, a constant ache that refused to subside. But now, as he looked at the camera, a glimmer of hope, a faint spark of light, began to flicker within him. The investigation, while harrowing, had also been a profound journey of self-discovery, a testament to the enduring power of love and the human spirit's capacity for resilience.

He had faced his demons, confronted his own vulnerabilities, and emerged stronger, more determined than ever to seek justice for those who had been wronged. The investigation had awakened a fierce resolve within him, a drive to uncover the truth, no matter how painful or uncomfortable it might be. He had learned that the pursuit of justice was not a linear path, but a winding, unpredictable journey, filled with obstacles and detours. He understood that justice and closure were not synonymous, that finding peace in the aftermath of tragedy was a complex and multifaceted process.

He had learned, too, the profound importance of forgiveness. Forgiving his sister's killer had not been an easy feat, but it had been a necessary step in his healing process. It had been a way to release himself from the shackles of anger and hatred, to reclaim his own sense of peace and serenity. He had learned that forgiveness was not about condoning the actions of the perpetrator, but about freeing himself from the burden of holding onto those negative emotions.

The investigation had also strengthened his bond with his family. They had shared his pain, his grief, and his frustration, offering their unwavering support and unconditional love. He realized that family was not just a collection of individuals bound by blood, but a tapestry woven with threads of love, compassion, and shared experiences. They had been there for him through the darkest of times, offering a lifeline of hope and a source of strength.

As John sat there, reflecting on the journey that had taken him from despair to hope, he knew that he would never forget his sister, Sarah. Her memory would forever be etched in his heart, a poignant reminder of the fragility of life and the enduring power of love. The vintage camera, the one that had captured the blurry photo, the one that had sparked a desperate search for answers, would remain a symbol of the truth that had been hidden for so long, a testament to the enduring power of love, compassion, and the human spirit's unwavering pursuit of justice. He would carry her memory with him always, honoring her legacy by striving for justice and seeking truth in all that he did.

The vintage camera, a relic of a time long gone, held a tangible link to Sarah's legacy. Its lens, once capturing fleeting moments of joy and laughter, now bore the weight of her final, tragic days. John kept it close, a constant reminder of her life, her disappearance, and the relentless pursuit of truth that had become his life's purpose.

The camera was a symbol, a testament to the power of a single image to expose hidden truths. It had become an emblem of the intricate web of deceit, the chilling reality of a long-lost sister's fate, and the enduring memory that would forever shape John's life. The blurred photograph within its frame, a ghostly glimpse into the past, was a testament to the power of evidence, even when it was fragmented and seemingly insignificant.

John found himself examining the camera often, tracing the contours of its worn metal, feeling the cool weight of its metal against his palm. It was as though he could sense Sarah's presence in its faded leather and the faint scent of time that clung to its body. Each time he looked through the lens, he saw not only the blurred image of her killer but also the reflection of his own journey – the pain of loss, the relentless pursuit of justice, and the enduring love for a sister whose absence he felt in the very core of his being.

The camera was a constant reminder of the weight of Sarah's case, a weight that had never truly lifted even after the capture of her killer. It reminded him of the relentless pursuit of truth, the painstaking process of unraveling layers of deception, and the unwavering belief in the power of justice that had guided his every step.

As he held the camera in his hand, he could almost hear the whispers of the past, the echoes of Sarah's laughter, the haunting silence of her disappearance, and the persistent voice of his own determination to find closure. The camera was a link to his sister, a bridge across the chasm of time, a vessel carrying the memories of a life that had been tragically cut short.

John knew that the camera would always hold a special place in his heart. It was a symbol of his commitment to seeking justice, a reminder of the enduring memory of his sister, and a testament to the unwavering belief in the power of truth that would forever guide his life. The camera, with its lens that captured the fleeting moments of life, had become a symbol of the enduring power of love, the unwavering pursuit of truth, and the profound impact of a sister's legacy on a brother's life.

The weight of Sarah's case had reshaped John, carving out a space within him that was reserved for her memory. The camera, a tangible link to his past, served as a constant reminder of the impact her disappearance had had on his life. It was a symbol of the enduring love that he felt for his sister, a love that transcended time, pain, and loss.

John's life had been irrevocably changed by Sarah's disappearance, a life marked by a relentless search for answers, a constant yearning for closure, and a profound sense of loss. The camera, a poignant symbol of his journey, served as a reminder of the impact his sister's life had had on his, a life that would forever be intertwined with her memory.

He knew that he would never be able to forget the pain of her absence, but he also knew that he would never truly let go of the love he felt for her. The camera, a precious memento of his sister's life, served as a constant reminder of the power of love, the relentless pursuit of truth, and the enduring legacy of a sister who would forever live on in his heart.

The camera, a physical embodiment of his journey, became a source of both pain and solace. It served as a reminder of the darkness that had shadowed his life, but also of the light that had guided him through it. The camera became a symbol of his unwavering commitment to finding justice, a symbol of his enduring love for his sister, and a symbol of his own personal journey towards healing and acceptance.

As John held the camera, he could almost hear Sarah's voice, whispering in his ear, reminding him of the importance of love, truth, and perseverance. The camera became a conduit, a connection to a world beyond the tangible, a world where memories lingered, love endured, and the pursuit of justice never truly ended.

John's life would forever be marked by the weight of his sister's absence, but he knew that her memory would also be a source of strength and inspiration. He carried her with him in his heart, in the photographs he treasured, in the stories he shared, and in the unwavering belief in the power of truth that would continue to guide his life. The camera, a symbol of his journey, served as a constant reminder of the enduring power of love, the relentless pursuit of justice, and the profound impact of a sister's legacy on a brother's life.

Chapter 6: The Whispers of the Past

The dream began with a familiar, chilling sound. It was Sarah's laugh, echoing through the empty halls of their childhood home. It wasn't a warm, joyful sound. It was hollow, tinged with a desperate, chilling edge that sent shivers down John's spine. He bolted awake, his heart pounding against his ribs, sweat slicking his skin. The room swam in the ghostly light of the rising sun, casting long, distorted shadows on the walls.

He tried to shake off the dream, but the memory of its unsettling reality clung to him like a shroud. In it, he was back in their childhood home, Sarah's favorite room – the one with the wide window overlooking the old willow tree – transformed into a scene of chaos. Furniture was overturned, and Sarah, her face pale and drawn, stood frozen in a pool of crimson. The air hung heavy with a metallic tang, and he could feel the weight of her silent scream pressing against his chest.

These visions, these haunting glimpses of Sarah's final moments, had begun subtly. A fleeting shadow in a crowded room, a whisper of her name on the wind. But they had grown increasingly vivid, disturbingly real. He could feel her cold hand on his, see her frantic eyes pleading for help. The line between reality and dream blurred, leaving him teetering on the precipice of sanity.

He wasn't sure if he was losing his grip on reality, or if the ghosts of the past were tightening their hold on him. He had spent years battling the demons of his sister's disappearance, burying the pain and guilt deep within him. But the investigation, the rediscovery of Sarah's case, had ripped open those wounds, leaving him raw and exposed.

He desperately wanted to believe that the nightmares were just his mind playing tricks, the consequence of sleep deprivation and the overwhelming burden of the case. But something deep within him whispered a different truth – a truth that sent a cold dread through him, making his blood run icy. He was being shown something, a truth that was hidden from him, a truth that could unlock the door to Sarah's final moments.

He couldn't ignore the whispers anymore. He had to face his fears, delve into the darkness that clung to his past, and uncover the truth that had been hidden for so long.

John sat at his desk, the vintage camera lying open on the surface. The blurry photograph, a testament to Sarah's final moments, stared back at him, a chilling reminder of the horror that had consumed his life. He had meticulously examined every detail, analyzed every shadow, but it had revealed no new answers.

He tried to focus on the investigation, on the tangible evidence he had gathered, but his mind kept drifting back to the dreams, the visions. He saw the shadowy figure, a fleeting image of Sarah's killer, but he still couldn't place the face, couldn't recognize the man who had taken his sister from him.

He closed his eyes, trying to calm his racing heart. He needed to find a way to control these visions, to decipher the messages they were desperately trying to convey. He was sure that the dreams held a key, a piece of the puzzle that had been missing for so long.

He decided to seek help. He had always been a man of logic, of reason, but this was beyond his control. He needed a professional, someone who could help him navigate the blurred lines between reality and the haunting grip of his past.

He listened as the phone rang, each ring echoing his own growing anxiety. He could hear Emily's voice, warm and calming, on the other end. She listened patiently as he explained his dreams, his fears, and the relentless hold that his past had on him.

"I understand," she said softly, her voice a balm to his troubled mind. "It's a common reaction for those who have experienced trauma. Your mind is trying to process the pain, to come to terms with what happened."

She listened intently as he described the visions, the unsettling details, and the growing sense of unease that had consumed him. She offered words of encouragement and advice, assuring him that he was not alone and that there was a way to navigate these dark waters.

"We need to find a way to understand these visions," she said. "They are trying to tell you something. It's up to us to decipher the language of your subconscious."

She suggested that he keep a journal, a way to record the visions in detail, to capture their essence and unravel the messages they held. She also suggested that he try visualization techniques, a way to confront his fears and to gain control over his thoughts and emotions.

John left the conversation feeling a sense of relief, a glimmer of hope amidst the shadows of his past. He had found a way to start the journey of healing, a way to reclaim his sanity and to find peace in the haunting grip of his sister's disappearance.

The next morning, John sat at his desk, his journal open before him, the vintage camera lying beside it. He took a deep breath, summoning his courage, and began to write. He poured his heart and soul onto the page, capturing the raw emotion, the vivid imagery, and the chilling details of his dreams.

He wrote about the haunted house, the overturned furniture, and Sarah's desperate cry for help. He wrote about the shadowy figure, the lingering sense of dread that followed him. He wrote about the fear, the confusion, and the relentless pursuit of answers that consumed him.

As he wrote, he felt a sense of release, a way to exorcise the demons that haunted him. He felt a connection to his sister, a shared pain that transcended the boundaries of life and death.

He began to see patterns in his visions, glimpses of a

hidden truth that was trying to break free from the depths of his subconscious. He focused on the details, the seemingly insignificant elements that had been dismissed as figments of his imagination. He realized that they held a key, a piece of the puzzle that could lead him to the truth.

He wrote about a single detail that had caught his attention, a detail that had been buried beneath the layers of fear and confusion. He saw a glimpse of a familiar object in the dream, a object that had been absent from the real crime scene. It was a small, wooden music box, a gift from Sarah to their younger brother, Tom, that had been missing for years.

This detail, this seemingly insignificant detail, sparked a fire within him. It was a thread, a faint glimmer of hope in the darkness, a possible connection between his dreams and reality.

He closed his journal, a sense of determination settling over him. He was not going to let these visions consume him. He was going to use them as a guide, a map to uncover the truth that had been hidden for so long.

He reached for the camera, the blurry photo staring back at him. He knew he had to find that music box, that missing piece of the puzzle, that link between his sister's disappearance and the secrets hidden in the shadows of his past.

He had to uncover the truth, no matter the cost, for his

sister, for himself, and for the haunting whispers from the past that were desperate to be heard.

John woke with a start, his heart pounding against his ribs like a trapped bird. The dream, or vision, was still vivid in his mind. It had been the same one for the past few nights, each time more intense, more unsettling. He saw Sarah, his sister, younger than he remembered, her hair a cascade of sun-kissed blonde, her laughter echoing in the summer air. But then, the image shifted, the vibrant hues turning to a sickly gray. He saw Sarah's terrified face, her eyes wide with fear as a shadowy figure loomed over her, the air thick with dread.

John sat up in bed, his breaths shallow and ragged. The dream was so real, so tangible, that for a moment he felt he could reach out and touch Sarah, feel her warmth. Then, the weight of reality settled upon him, heavy and cold. Sarah was gone, her life snuffed out before its time. He had finally caught her killer, or so he thought. But these dreams, these visions, were chipping away at his certainty, casting a doubt that felt like a dark cloud hovering over him.

He was haunted by the image of David, his confession ringing in his ears. He had admitted to stalking Sarah, taking photos of her without her knowledge, his obsession growing into a terrifying darkness. He had confessed to killing her, the details of the crime chillingly vivid. Yet, something felt wrong. There was a discordance, a dissonance in his gut that he couldn't ignore.

The vision he'd had – the shadowy figure, the terrifying air of menace – didn't quite fit the profile of David, who was more of a withdrawn, isolated man, consumed by his own anxieties and desires. There was a coldness, a calculating malice to the figure in the vision that didn't align with David's seemingly meek demeanor.

John ran a hand through his hair, his thoughts swirling in a dizzying vortex. Could he have been wrong all along? Could David be protecting someone else, shielding a more sinister presence from the light of justice? His heart pounded in his chest, a drumbeat of growing suspicion.

He couldn't shake off the feeling that something was amiss, that a crucial piece of the puzzle was still missing. He knew he had to revisit the investigation, scrutinize every detail, every piece of evidence, seeking answers to the nagging doubts that were gnawing at him.

He spent the next few days going over the case files, meticulously studying every piece of evidence, every witness statement. He focused on David's confession, searching for inconsistencies, hidden agendas. He reread the reports, each page a haunting reminder of Sarah's tragic fate. But as he delved deeper into the case, the more he questioned the truth of David's confession.

John found himself questioning every detail, every statement. He examined David's alibi, the timeline of his actions, his motive for killing Sarah. His initial conviction in David's guilt was slowly crumbling, replaced by a growing sense of unease.

He focused on the inconsistencies in David's confession. He had claimed to act alone, yet his description of the crime scene, his knowledge of Sarah's movements, seemed too detailed, too precise, as if he had been privy to information only someone else could have known.

John's mind was a tangle of suspicions and possibilities. He remembered the blurry photo, the only glimpse they had of the killer. It was the photo that had led them to David, a key piece of evidence that had seemingly sealed his fate. Yet, he couldn't help but wonder if the photo had misled them. Could it have been manipulated, designed to point them towards a false culprit? He remembered the forensic artist's composite sketch, based on the blurry photo. He pulled out the file, his fingers tracing the outline of the face, the faint tattoo on the wrist. It was that tattoo that had been the defining feature, leading them to Emily, who, it turned out, had been falsely accused.

John's mind raced with possibilities, a jumble of doubts and suspicions. He felt like he was on the edge of a precipice, the ground unsteady beneath him. He needed answers, concrete evidence to confirm his suspicions, to prove that he hadn't been wrong, that his intuition wasn't playing tricks on him. He couldn't afford to ignore this growing feeling, this gut-wrenching sense of unease that was slowly consuming him.

He knew he had to revisit the crime scene, seek out clues that had been overlooked, fragments of evidence that had been missed during the initial investigation. He had to find something, anything, to prove that there was more to the case, that something wasn't adding up. His determination was a fiery torch, burning away the doubts and insecurities that threatened to consume him. He was driven by a need for truth, a relentless pursuit of justice, not just for his sister, but for everyone who had been wronged.

His journey was far from over, the whispers of the past echoing in his ears, a constant reminder of the shadows that lurked in the corners of his mind. He was ready to face the truth, no matter how unsettling, how painful. He would unravel the secrets, expose the lies, and find the answers he sought. His sister's memory demanded it. His own sanity demanded it. He would find the truth, even if it meant confronting his own fears and doubts. He would fight for the truth, even if it meant facing the darkness that threatened to consume him. His sister's case was far from closed. The shadows of doubt, the whispers of the past, were not going to be silenced. The quest for truth, for justice, was just beginning.

The air in the old, abandoned warehouse felt heavy with the silence of years. John Snider, his face etched with the weariness of a man who had spent decades chasing ghosts, stood in the center of the cold, concrete floor, his gaze fixed on the spot where Sarah's body had been found. The fluorescent lights overhead cast an eerie glow, illuminating the dust motes that danced in the air like miniature ghosts. He ran his hand along the rough concrete wall, feeling the chill seep through his gloves. It had been years since he had last stood in this place, years since he had seen the evidence of his sister's disappearance.

He had always blamed himself for not being able to protect Sarah. He had been a young detective then, inexperienced and naive, overwhelmed by the enormity of his sister's disappearance. He had let the case slip through his fingers, a mistake he carried with him every day.

He had come back here, not for closure, but for answers. The whispers of the past had begun to echo in his dreams, unsettling and persistent. The confession of David, Sarah's supposed killer, had seemed so clear, so conclusive. Yet, the doubts gnawed at him, the whispers of a truth yet to be revealed. David's story had felt incomplete, a carefully constructed narrative meant to conceal the truth.

John pulled out his notepad, the worn pages filled with notes, sketches, and timelines, a tangible reminder of his relentless pursuit of justice. He scrutinized every detail of the crime scene, his eyes darting over the floor, the walls, the faded paint, looking for clues that had been overlooked. He noticed a small, faded stain near the wall, barely visible to the naked eye. He knelt down, carefully examining the stain. It was a faint brown, barely noticeable, but something about it felt different. It didn't seem to belong. He reached for his flashlight, its beam illuminating the stain in a new light. It was a trace of blood, dried and almost invisible.

He knew that the initial investigation had not focused on this area, and the blood had likely been missed. This small, seemingly insignificant detail, sparked a flicker of hope in John's heart. It was a clue, a piece of the puzzle that could lead him closer to the truth. He carefully collected a sample of the blood, sealing it in a plastic bag, a sense of purpose returning to his weary soul.

He studied the photographs of the crime scene, his gaze lingering on the details, trying to find any inconsistencies, any hints of a story that had been silenced. He focused on the area where the bloodstain had been discovered, realizing that it was positioned in an odd spot. It was too far away from the area where the body had been found.

He realized that this was not a simple case of a struggle, a hasty crime of passion. This was a planned act, a calculated move, a deliberate choice of location. It was a crime that had been carefully orchestrated, designed to mislead the investigation.

John traced the path of the bloodstain with his finger, visualizing the events that had transpired. He realized that it had likely been left by someone who had been carrying Sarah's body, someone who had been at the scene during the actual crime, someone who had been involved in the actual abduction. The blood had been transferred from Sarah's body to the person who had carried her. The question was, who was this person?

He remembered David's confession, his claim that he had

been alone with Sarah during the abduction. But John knew better. There was something about David's story that didn't ring true. The bloodstain, its position, its significance, all pointed to a different truth.

He reviewed the evidence, the photographs, the witness statements, the reports. He pieced together the puzzle, the fragments of information, the inconsistencies, the details that had been ignored, the voices of the past that whispered in the shadows. He began to see the truth, a truth that David had tried to bury. The truth that someone else had been involved in Sarah's disappearance, someone who had been working in the shadows, someone who had been deliberately manipulating the events.

John knew he needed to find this person, to uncover the truth that had been concealed for so long. He felt a renewed sense of determination, a fire rekindled in his soul. He was no longer just a detective chasing ghosts, he was a man on a mission, a mission to avenge his sister's death, to bring the real killers to justice.

John sat at his desk, the vintage camera resting on a stack of files. The blurry photo, a ghostly testament to Sarah's final moments, stared back at him, its silence deafening. He had spent weeks poring over it, analyzing every pixel, seeking a clue, a whisper of the past that might unlock the mystery. David's confession had been a breakthrough, but it felt incomplete, a puzzle with missing pieces. Something about David's account, the way he described the events, the lack of detail, the subtle inconsistencies, it all felt off. He had accepted the confession, brought closure to the family, but a nagging doubt persisted. He had a gut feeling that the truth wasn't entirely revealed.

The more he thought about it, the more inconsistencies emerged. David's alibi, for instance. He claimed to be at a friend's house on the night Sarah disappeared, a seemingly solid alibi. But John had a hard time accepting it. He knew David, or at least he thought he did. David was a quiet, reserved individual, someone who kept to himself, not the type to be out socializing on a Friday night. Then there was the matter of motive. David's confession mentioned a fleeting resentment, a jealousy fueled by Sarah's attention to another man. It felt contrived, a flimsy excuse, something that didn't ring true. John knew there was more to it, a deeper motive that David was concealing.

He decided to delve deeper into David's life, revisiting the evidence he had gathered, searching for any overlooked detail, any hidden clue that might lead him to the missing pieces of the puzzle. His investigation led him to a forgotten box of personal belongings, a collection of mementos, photographs, and letters that David had kept hidden away. Among them, he found a small, leather-bound diary, its pages filled with cryptic notes and sketches. It was a record of David's thoughts, his fears, his desires. It was an intimate window into his mind, a glimpse into his hidden world.

The diary revealed a side of David that John had never

imagined. It spoke of a deep-seated obsession, a twisted love bordering on madness. David was infatuated with Sarah, his feelings growing stronger with every passing day. He had secretly stalked her, photographing her without her knowledge, his obsession building into a desperate need to possess her. But the diary also mentioned another person, someone who held the key to David's true motive. It was a woman, a woman David had been involved with, someone who had vanished without a trace shortly after Sarah's disappearance.

John's heart pounded as he read the diary, a sense of urgency gripping him. The woman's name was Emily, and she was not just any woman; she was a former colleague of David's, someone who had worked alongside him at a local photography studio. He knew he had to find Emily, to learn about her connection to David and Sarah, to understand their relationship and its potential impact on the case. He knew that this woman held the missing pieces of the puzzle, the key to unraveling the truth behind Sarah's disappearance.

The hunt for Emily was a race against time. She had vanished without a trace, leaving behind a trail of cryptic clues that led John on a relentless pursuit. He followed every lead, every whisper of her existence, desperate to find her and uncover the truth she held. He retraced her steps, spoke to people who knew her, pieced together fragments of her life, trying to understand her motives and her connection to David and Sarah.

He learned that Emily had been a gifted photographer, a

talented artist with a passion for capturing the beauty of the world. But she was also a troubled soul, tormented by a dark secret that had consumed her life. Her relationship with David had been turbulent, a passionate affair fueled by an obsession that turned toxic. David had been possessive, jealous, and controlling, his love turning into a dangerous obsession that had driven Emily to the brink.

John discovered that Emily had been the one to take the blurry photograph, the photograph that had become the central piece of evidence in the case. She had been present on the night Sarah disappeared, a silent witness to the events that had unfolded. She had been drawn into David's web of obsession, forced to participate in his twisted game. But she had also been trapped in a web of her own, a victim of David's manipulations, her own secrets weighing heavily on her soul.

As John dug deeper, he uncovered a series of events that had taken place shortly before Sarah's disappearance, events that had pushed Emily to her breaking point. David had threatened Emily, his jealousy reaching a fever pitch, his obsession turning dangerous. He had warned her to stay away from Sarah, to stop interfering in his life. He had threatened to expose her secrets, to ruin her life if she did not obey him. The pressure had become too much, the weight of her secrets too heavy to bear. Emily had made a desperate decision, a decision that had forever changed her life and had led to Sarah's disappearance.

John realized that Emily had been playing a dangerous game, caught in a web of lies and deceit, her own secrets blurring the lines between truth and deception. He knew that she had been involved in the events that had unfolded, but he was still trying to understand her role, her motives, and her connection to Sarah's disappearance. He knew that the truth was a tangled web, a tapestry woven with secrets and lies, and he was determined to unravel it, to find the missing pieces that would finally bring closure to the case.

He confronted Emily with the evidence he had gathered, her secrets laid bare, her lies unraveling. She had been living a double life, her true self hidden behind a carefully constructed facade. She had been caught in a web of her own making, her decisions driven by a desperation that had led her down a path of darkness. She admitted to her involvement in Sarah's disappearance, her guilt overwhelming her, her heart heavy with the burden of her actions.

She confessed that she had been present on the night Sarah disappeared, that she had witnessed the events that had unfolded. She had been there when David had taken Sarah to the abandoned warehouse, her presence a chilling testament to the dark depths of their relationship. She had been forced to participate in David's twisted game, her own secrets and fears holding her hostage. But she had also been a silent witness to David's true motive, a motive that went beyond jealousy and obsession.

Emily revealed that David had not acted alone, that there was another person involved, someone who had orchestrated the events from the shadows, someone who had used David as a pawn in a larger scheme. She confessed that David had been blackmailed, forced to act against his will, his secrets and vulnerabilities exploited for someone else's gain. She was the key to unlocking this hidden truth, the missing piece that would unravel the larger conspiracy that had led to Sarah's disappearance.

John was stunned by Emily's revelation. The case had taken a new turn, the investigation entering uncharted territory. He realized that he had been focusing on the wrong people, that the truth was far more intricate, far more sinister than he had ever imagined. The case had become a tangled web of secrets, betrayals, and hidden motives, a labyrinth of deceit that he needed to unravel. He was determined to expose the truth, no matter the cost, to bring justice to Sarah's memory and to those who had been caught in the web of this conspiracy.

The case had become a quest for the truth, a relentless pursuit of justice that would lead John on a perilous journey. He was facing a powerful adversary, an organization shrouded in secrecy, an entity that operated in the shadows, manipulating events and controlling lives. He knew that he was taking a significant risk, that he was walking a dangerous path. But he was determined to expose the truth, to hold those responsible accountable, to bring closure to the case that had haunted him for so long. He knew that the truth would be costly, but he was willing to pay the price, to face the consequences, to fight for justice, for his sister, and for those who had been wronged. The pursuit of truth had become his mission, his destiny, and he was not going to give up until the truth was revealed, no matter the cost.

John found himself staring at the composite sketch of David, the man who confessed to Sarah's murder. He had a strange feeling in his gut, a feeling that there was more to the story than David had revealed. His confession had seemed too easy, too clean, like a carefully crafted script designed to deflect attention.

John knew that David had a history of violence, a tendency towards obsessive behavior, but he couldn't shake the feeling that there was another player in this game, someone who had masterminded the whole thing. David might have been a pawn, a willing pawn, but a pawn nonetheless.

John delved into David's life, his past, and his connections. He reviewed the evidence once more, scrutinizing every detail, looking for any anomaly, anything that could reveal a hidden agenda, a conspirator lurking in the shadows.

His investigation led him to David's workplace, a local photography studio. John knew that David had been secretly taking pictures of Sarah, documenting his obsession, his pursuit. But were those photographs just a personal indulgence, or were they a part of a bigger scheme?

John spoke to the studio owner, a man who seemed to be genuinely shaken by the revelations about David's actions. He had been oblivious to David's obsession with Sarah, unaware of the sinister photographs he had been taking. But there was something else, something unspoken, a hint of fear in his eyes, a guardedness that hinted at a hidden truth.

John pressed further, pushing through the owner's reluctance. He learned that David had been working on a special project, a photo essay about Sarah, meticulously documenting her life, her movements, her routines. But why? What was the purpose of this obsession, this relentless documentation?

The answer lay in a hidden drawer in the studio's back office, a drawer that David had meticulously locked and hidden from everyone. Inside, John found a series of photographs, not the usual candid shots of Sarah, but a series of photographs that revealed a chilling truth.

The photographs showed Sarah in various locations, her movements captured by a hidden camera. She was unaware, oblivious to the fact that someone was watching her, documenting her life, tracing her every step. John's stomach churned as he realized the extent of David's obsession.

There was a pattern to the photographs, a methodical progression, like a carefully orchestrated plan. Each photograph captured Sarah at a specific location, at a specific time, a timeline that revealed the details of

David's meticulous planning.

John felt a cold shiver run down his spine as he recognized the locations in the photographs. They were the same locations that Sarah had mentioned in her last conversation with John, the locations where she had felt a sense of unease, a sense of being watched.

The photographs were more than just a documentation of David's obsession, they were a map, a roadmap to his sinister plan. He had been tracking Sarah, preparing for his ultimate act, a plan he had meticulously executed, leaving no trace, no evidence.

John knew he needed to dig deeper, to find the missing piece, the piece that could connect David's obsession to his ultimate act. There had to be a reason behind his meticulously planned act, a motive that drove his obsession, his relentless pursuit.

He scrutinized the photographs again, searching for any clues, any anomaly that could reveal the missing piece. He noticed that there was a small detail in some of the photographs, a detail that had been overlooked in the initial investigation.

It was a subtle detail, barely noticeable at first glance, but it was enough to ignite a spark of hope in John's mind. In some of the photographs, there was a faint outline, a blurry image of a shadowy figure lurking in the background, a figure that was not David.

This figure, barely discernible, was a ghost in the photographs, a phantom that seemed to be watching Sarah, observing her, almost guiding David's actions. It was a faint clue, a whisper from the past, but it was enough to open a new chapter in John's investigation.

Who was this figure? Why was he lurking in the shadows? What was his connection to David, to Sarah?

John knew he had to follow this new lead, to unravel the mystery behind this ghostly figure, to find the missing piece that could finally reveal the truth behind Sarah's disappearance. He was determined to unearth the secrets of the past, to confront the ghosts that had haunted him for years, and to finally find the justice his sister deserved.

Chapter 7: The Unveiled Truth

John's investigation had led him down a rabbit hole, a labyrinth of deceit and betrayal. The more he uncovered, the more he realized the truth was a moving target, constantly shifting and revealing itself in fragments. He had discovered David's confession was riddled with inconsistencies, and the weight of the evidence pointed towards a deeper, darker truth.

It was during one of his late-night research sessions that John stumbled upon a name – Peter. A former colleague of David's, Peter had been involved in a business deal with Sarah's company several years ago. The deal had gone sour, leaving a bitter aftertaste in Peter's mouth. John had always been aware of Peter's presence in the periphery of his investigation, but he had never considered him a serious suspect. After all, Peter had a solid alibi, a seemingly clean past, and no obvious connection to Sarah.

But as John delved deeper, he began to unearth a pattern of suspicious activity. Peter had been suspiciously quiet about Sarah's disappearance, and his responses to John's inquiries had been evasive and guarded. It was as if he was holding back something, a secret that was slowly gnawing at him.

John's suspicions were confirmed when he discovered a series of financial transactions between Peter and David.

The transactions, shrouded in secrecy, suggested a hidden agreement, a pact of silence that had been forged between the two men. John's intuition told him that Peter was hiding something, something that could potentially link him to Sarah's disappearance.

He decided to delve into Peter's past, meticulously combing through his financial records, business ventures, and personal relationships. It was a painstaking process, a relentless pursuit of the truth that was hidden beneath layers of lies and deception.

John's efforts eventually paid off when he stumbled upon a series of financial irregularities, a trail of hidden funds and fraudulent activities that Peter had meticulously concealed. The irregularities revealed a complex web of corruption, a scheme that Peter had orchestrated to defraud investors and steal millions of dollars.

The truth was a bitter pill to swallow. John realized that Peter had been involved in a series of financial crimes, and Sarah had been on the verge of exposing his schemes. She had threatened to reveal his corruption, jeopardizing his carefully constructed empire of deceit. This revelation provided a motive for Peter to have wanted Sarah out of the picture.

John's investigation took on a new urgency. He had to gather irrefutable evidence to prove Peter's guilt and unravel the truth behind Sarah's disappearance. He focused his efforts on establishing a direct connection between Peter and the crime scene, a link that would definitively tie him to Sarah's abduction.

After weeks of meticulous research, John discovered a crucial piece of evidence – a single, inconspicuous receipt found hidden in the back of Peter's car. The receipt was from a convenience store located just a few blocks from where Sarah's body had been discovered. John had checked the store's surveillance footage, and the footage revealed a man matching Peter's description purchasing items on the day Sarah went missing.

The evidence was undeniable, a smoking gun that pointed directly to Peter's involvement. John knew he had to act quickly to apprehend Peter and bring him to justice. He had spent years searching for the truth, for answers to the haunting mystery of his sister's disappearance. Now, he was finally closing in on the killer.

John felt a surge of adrenaline course through his veins as he prepared to confront Peter. The weight of years of frustration and grief had coalesced into a resolute determination to expose the truth, to bring closure to his sister's case, and to seek justice for the victim. He would not let Peter escape, he would not allow the darkness of deceit to triumph over the light of truth.

He gathered his evidence, meticulously reviewed his findings, and prepared for a final confrontation. John had faced countless criminals in his career, but this case was different. This case was personal. This case was about his sister.

The confrontation with Peter would not be easy. Peter was a cunning manipulator, a master of deception who had successfully evaded justice for years. John knew he had to be prepared for a long and arduous battle, a fight that would require every ounce of his skill, determination, and courage. But John was ready. He had come too far, he had endured too much, to allow the truth to be buried again.

The truth was a powerful force, a light that could pierce through the darkest of shadows. John knew that if he could expose the truth, he could bring solace to Sarah's memory and find a measure of peace within himself. He would never forget the scars of the past, but he hoped that by uncovering the truth, he could find a path to healing and a sense of justice that had eluded him for so long. The pursuit of truth was a relentless pursuit, a quest for closure that would require every ounce of his strength, determination, and will. But John was prepared to face the challenge, to fight for justice, and to finally bring the truth to light.

John's pursuit of truth led him to Peter, a man shrouded in an air of affluence and respectability. Peter had been a colleague of David, and their paths had crossed during Sarah's disappearance. While David had been dismissed as a disgruntled ex-employee, John felt a gnawing unease. There was something about Peter, a certain calculating coldness in his demeanor that hinted at a deeper involvement.

John's intuition was confirmed when he uncovered a

series of financial transactions between Peter and David. The transactions were suspicious, hinting at a secret agreement, a cover-up. John dug deeper, piecing together a mosaic of evidence that revealed a disturbing reality. Peter had been involved in a string of financial crimes, skimming money from clients, manipulating investments, and exploiting loopholes in the system.

The revelation sent a tremor through John, a chilling realization. Sarah had been investigating Peter's financial crimes, threatening to expose his illicit activities. It was this threat, John suspected, that had led Peter to silence her. He had arranged for David, with his violent past and tendency to lash out, to take the fall. It was a calculated move, a cold-blooded act of self-preservation disguised as a desperate attempt to protect his reputation.

The weight of this revelation bore down on John. It wasn't just the betrayal of a friend, the cold-hearted manipulation of another person's life. It was a deeper betrayal, a violation of trust, a reminder of the depths of human corruption. It was a reflection of the darkness that lurked beneath the veneer of respectability, the secrets that festered in the shadows.

John needed to confront Peter, to present him with the evidence he had gathered. He needed to expose the truth, to hold him accountable for his actions. But John knew this was a dangerous game, a game where the stakes were high. Peter wouldn't go down without a fight. He was cunning, resourceful, and had a network of influence that extended far beyond the scope of John's investigation.

John's investigation had taken on a new urgency. He was no longer just chasing the ghosts of the past, he was hunting a predator, a man who had orchestrated Sarah's disappearance, who had manipulated the lives of others for his own gain. He was playing against a formidable adversary, a man who moved with the grace of a viper, leaving a trail of deceit and destruction in his wake.

John's determination to expose Peter's crimes was fueled by a mix of grief, anger, and a yearning for justice. He had to bring this man down, not only for his sister but for all the victims Peter had wronged. He had to expose the truth, no matter the cost.

The evidence was mounting, a dam about to burst. John knew he was close. He had to be careful, however, not to expose himself or risk jeopardizing his investigation. The stakes were too high, and he couldn't afford to make a mistake.

John's path to justice was fraught with danger. He found himself navigating a treacherous landscape of deceit, manipulation, and hidden agendas. He had to tread carefully, staying one step ahead of Peter, always anticipating his next move. The clock was ticking, and time was running out.

John's determination was unwavering. He had spent years searching for the truth, and he was determined to find it. He would not rest until he had exposed Peter's crimes and brought him to justice. His quest was not just for Sarah, but for everyone who had been hurt by Peter's deceit.

He sought to unravel Peter's intricate web of lies, to expose the true motives behind the secret agreement, and to understand the depths of Peter's depravity. He had to find the missing pieces, to complete the puzzle, to unveil the truth.

John was not just a detective, he was a warrior, a crusader for justice, fighting against the forces of darkness. His mission was to expose the truth, no matter the cost. He was on a journey of redemption, a journey to find peace for himself and to bring justice to his sister's memory.

He knew he could not bring Sarah back, but he could bring Peter to justice. He could expose the truth, no matter how painful it was. He could hold this man accountable for his actions, and in doing so, he could bring a measure of closure to his own grief.

The road ahead was treacherous, but John was prepared. He was ready to face whatever came his way, to confront the darkness and bring light to the truth. He was determined to uncover the web of connections that had led to Sarah's disappearance, to bring Peter to justice, and to honor his sister's memory by fighting for a world where truth and justice prevailed.

John stood in Peter's opulent office, the scent of expensive leather and polished wood assaulting his senses. A tension hung heavy in the air, palpable and oppressive. He placed a worn, leather-bound folder on the desk, its edges slightly worn from the countless times he'd flipped through it. Peter's face, normally a mask of smooth confidence, was now etched with a barely-concealed panic.

"Peter," John began, his voice calm but firm, "We've been going over the evidence, and it's become increasingly clear that you played a significant role in Sarah's disappearance."

John watched as Peter's gaze darted around the room, his hands nervously twisting a silver pen.

"I don't understand what you're implying, John," Peter said, his voice tight. "You know I've been nothing but cooperative with this investigation. I've given you every bit of information I could."

"That's true," John admitted. "You've been very cooperative. Too cooperative, perhaps. You've been too eager to prove your innocence, which makes me wonder if you're hiding something."

John took a slow, deliberate breath, his mind racing through the details he'd painstakingly pieced together. He had a compelling case, a tapestry woven from countless threads of evidence, but he knew Peter was a cunning man, adept at weaving his own intricate webs of deceit.

He began to lay out the evidence, his voice measured and calm, each detail a blow to Peter's carefully constructed facade. He spoke of the financial discrepancies, the suspicious transactions, the sudden influx of wealth that coincided with Sarah's disappearance. He mentioned the forged documents, the hidden accounts, the elaborate network of deceit that Peter had meticulously built.

"Your relationship with David wasn't just a business partnership," John said, watching Peter's face pale. "You used him, manipulated him, made him take the blame for your crimes. You were the one who wanted Sarah out of the picture, weren't you?"

Peter remained silent, his eyes wide and filled with a mixture of fear and defiance.

"You were terrified of Sarah exposing your illicit activities," John pressed. "She was a threat to your carefully constructed empire. You needed to silence her. You wanted her gone. You were willing to do anything to protect yourself."

John knew he needed more, something tangible, something that would shatter Peter's denials and force him to confront the truth.

"You're a smart man, Peter," John continued, leaning forward, "and you've done a brilliant job of covering your tracks. But you overlooked a crucial detail. A detail that links you to the scene of the crime."

He unfolded a photograph from the folder, placing it on the desk in front of Peter. It was a grainy, blurry image, captured from a security camera overlooking the abandoned warehouse where Sarah's body was discovered. The image was dark and obscured, but it was clear enough to reveal a figure, a figure that John recognized.

"That's you, Peter," John said, his voice steady. "This was taken on the night of Sarah's disappearance. You were at the warehouse. And you weren't there alone. "

John felt a surge of adrenaline, a rush of determination. He had Peter cornered, his carefully woven facade crumbling under the weight of the truth. He needed to keep pushing, to make Peter crack, to force him to reveal everything.

"You were desperate," John said, his voice resonating with conviction. "You were willing to do anything to protect your empire. You were willing to sacrifice Sarah. But I won't let you get away with it. I won't let her memory be tarnished by your lies."

As John spoke, the weight of years of unfulfilled justice and agonizing grief surged through him. He had spent decades searching for the truth, haunted by the memory of his sister, the empty space she left behind. Now, with this final piece of evidence, he could finally face Peter, the man who had stolen Sarah's life and broken their family.

The air in the office crackled with tension, the silence punctuated only by Peter's ragged breaths. He stared at the photograph, his eyes darting back and forth between the image and John's face. 128

"You're wrong, John," Peter finally whispered, his voice trembling. "You have the wrong man."

But John knew he had him. The truth was starting to unravel, the threads of Peter's carefully constructed web coming loose. The pursuit of justice had been long and arduous, but he wouldn't stop now. He would expose Peter for who he truly was, and he would finally bring Sarah's story to a close.

John's pursuit of justice had taken him on a harrowing journey, a labyrinthine path filled with deception, betrayal, and the weight of a long-lost sister's unsolved disappearance. He had endured sleepless nights, agonizing doubts, and the constant fear of failure. But he refused to surrender, driven by a deep-seated belief in truth and a relentless pursuit of justice for his sister, Sarah.

The evidence he had gathered was a tapestry woven from countless threads – financial discrepancies, hidden accounts, forged documents, and now, the blurry image that linked Peter to the crime scene. It was the culmination of years of tireless investigation, a relentless pursuit of the truth.

Now, he stood on the precipice of truth, with Peter's carefully constructed facade crumbling under the weight of his own deception. But John knew that even as he confronted Peter, there would be no real closure. The pain of Sarah's absence would remain a constant ache in his heart, a reminder of the enduring legacy of loss.

John knew the fight wasn't over. He had to confront Peter, to force him to confess, to expose the truth. But he also knew that the journey had changed him. He had faced his fears, his doubts, and his grief. He had unearthed the secrets of the past and uncovered a web of corruption and deceit. But through it all, he had emerged stronger, more resolute, and more determined to find justice.

He took a deep breath, steeled his resolve, and prepared to face the man who had taken Sarah from him. He would expose Peter, bring him to justice, and finally find a sliver of peace. He would do it for Sarah, for the sister he loved, for the truth he had relentlessly pursued, and for the justice he had fought so hard to achieve.

John's relentless pursuit of truth had led him to Peter, a former colleague of David. The trail of hidden funds and fraudulent activities Peter had been involved in had long been a whisper in the corridors of the financial world. John had meticulously pieced together the puzzle, unearthing a string of shady business deals, and unearthed a web of deceit that intertwined with the disappearance of Sarah. He was determined to uncover the truth, no matter the cost.

The key to unraveling Peter's involvement lay in his meticulously kept financial records, hidden away in a secure offshore account. John, with the help of a trusted forensic accountant, delved into Peter's finances, uncovering a trail of hidden funds and fraudulent activities that had been meticulously concealed for years. His investigation revealed a pattern of illicit transactions, shell corporations, and offshore accounts, all designed to launder money and evade taxes. The accountant's report detailed a complex network of financial maneuvers, each meticulously crafted to obscure the true source of the funds.

The pieces of the puzzle began to fit together. John had been following the wrong path, misled by David's confession, which now seemed to be a carefully crafted facade. The truth was that David had been the scapegoat, an unwitting pawn in Peter's carefully orchestrated scheme. Peter had orchestrated Sarah's disappearance to silence her, a threat to his illicit empire.

One crucial document, a seemingly innocuous bank transfer slip, became the cornerstone of John's case. It was a transfer of a large sum of money, sent from Peter's offshore account to a seemingly unrelated bank account in a neighboring state. John meticulously cross-referenced the account details, discovering that the recipient of the funds was a company that owned a small but secluded cottage on the outskirts of town, a location that was eerily similar to the one where Sarah's skeleton was found.

John's mind raced. The evidence was mounting, pointing directly at Peter. He remembered the day Sarah had disappeared, a day when she had been scheduled to meet with Peter to discuss a financial discrepancy she had discovered. The evidence suggested that Peter had lured Sarah to the secluded cottage, where he had silenced her permanently, framing David for his crime.

John needed to confirm his suspicions. He sought out the owner of the cottage, a reclusive woman who had been living there for years, seemingly oblivious to the events that had transpired in her humble abode. Through careful questioning and a meticulous search of the cottage, John uncovered crucial evidence - a single, tiny piece of jewelry, a pendant that Sarah had been wearing the day she vanished. It was a small but significant detail, linking Peter directly to the crime scene.

With his investigation nearing its climax, John felt a surge of adrenaline mingled with a sense of foreboding. He had spent months chasing shadows, plagued by doubts and uncertainties. Now, finally, he had a concrete piece of evidence that would expose Peter's heinous crime. He knew that confronting Peter would be a dangerous encounter, a confrontation that could change the course of their lives.

With the weight of his sister's memory heavy on his shoulders, John knew he had to confront Peter. He had to bring justice to Sarah, even if it meant risking his own life. He had spent months chasing shadows, and now, with the weight of his sister's memory heavy on his shoulders, he was ready to face the truth. The final evidence, a tiny pendant recovered from the cottage, was the missing piece of the puzzle, the key that would unlock the truth behind Sarah's disappearance. The final confrontation with Peter was inevitable, a battle that would determine the fate of both their lives.

The weight of the evidence hung heavy in the air between John and Peter. The truth, like a dark cloud, had settled over the room, suffocating any pretense of innocence. John, his face etched with the years of searching, met Peter's gaze, his eyes reflecting the pain and anger that had been simmering within him for decades.

"Peter," John began, his voice strained with emotion, "I have the proof. You were there that night. You were the one who lured Sarah away, the one who took her life. All those years, you hid in the shadows, manipulating events, using David as your shield. But you won't get away with it anymore."

Peter's face contorted with a mixture of fear and defiance. He tried to maintain a façade of composure, but the tremor in his voice betrayed him. He desperately attempted to cling to a shred of deniability, his eyes darting around the room, searching for an escape from the truth that was closing in on him.

"John," he stammered, his voice cracking, "you're wrong. This is all a misunderstanding. I had nothing to do with Sarah's disappearance."

John scoffed, the evidence he had gathered overwhelming and irrefutable. "Don't play games with me, Peter. I've been through every shred of evidence, every detail, every twisted story. And I know what you did. You made David your pawn, a scapegoat to take the fall for your crimes. But I saw through the charade. I knew there was something more, something darker behind David's actions."

John recounted the evidence he had gathered, a tapestry of interconnected clues that painted a harrowing picture of Peter's involvement. He spoke of the financial irregularities, the fraudulent transactions, the hidden accounts that pointed directly to Peter's desperate need for money – a need he believed Sarah had threatened to expose.

"You were drowning in debt, Peter. Sarah was about to bring down your empire. You couldn't let that happen, could you? So, you took her away, silenced her forever, and used David to cover your tracks."

Peter, cornered, finally cracked. The facade of innocence crumbled, leaving behind a man consumed by desperation and guilt. His eyes, once cold and calculating, now held a flicker of fear, a faint recognition of his impending doom.

"It's true," Peter whispered, his voice barely audible. "But it wasn't planned. It wasn't supposed to happen like this. It was an accident."

"An accident?" John countered, his voice sharp with disbelief. "You call taking a life, deliberately silencing a woman who was about to expose your crimes, an accident? There was nothing accidental about it, Peter. You were driven by greed, by a desperate need to protect your own skin."

John's words pierced through Peter's carefully constructed facade of self-deception. He realized the futility of his attempts to deny the truth, to cling to a semblance of innocence. The weight of his actions, the consequences of his choices, had finally caught up with him.

"I just needed to protect myself," Peter pleaded, his voice laced with desperation. "Sarah was going to ruin me. I had a family to protect, a life to maintain."

"At what cost, Peter?" John countered, his voice filled with a quiet fury. "At the cost of a life? A sister, a daughter, a friend? You stole everything from her, everything from us. You left us with nothing but the bitter taste of betrayal and the haunting memory of her loss."

Peter, defeated, could only offer a feeble apology, a hollow gesture that held no weight in the face of the devastation he had caused. He had been trapped in his web of lies, his self-preservation eclipsing any sense of morality, any shred of humanity. He had forgotten that behind the façade of his carefully constructed world, a real person, a woman he had known and interacted with, had lost her life, her future, her dreams.

As the truth unravelled, as the weight of Peter's confession settled on the room, John finally felt a sliver of closure. He had brought his sister's killer to justice, but the pain of her loss remained, an indelible mark on his soul. He realized that while justice had been served, it could never truly mend the shattered pieces of his heart, the wounds inflicted by the cruel twist of fate that had taken his sister away.

Chapter 8: The Aftermath

The weight of truth pressed down on John, a heavy cloak of exhaustion and disillusionment. The culmination of the investigation, the exposure of Peter's crimes, had brought a sense of relief, a validation of years of agonizing uncertainty. But it had also left him drained, his spirit sapped by the relentless pursuit of justice, the unyielding need to uncover the truth, even when it was painful to face.

He realized that the truth, once revealed, was like a jagged shard of glass. It could cut deeply, leaving wounds that were slow to heal. The process of uncovering it had been emotionally draining, a relentless journey through a labyrinth of secrets and lies. He had delved into the darkest corners of his family's past, unearthed long-buried resentments and secrets, and confronted the fragility of human nature.

The weight of Sarah's death, the realization that her killer had been living among them for years, was a burden that John carried with a profound sense of sorrow. He had sought justice, but it had come at a cost, leaving him with the knowledge that his sister's life had been stolen, that the laughter and joy she had brought to their lives had been brutally extinguished.

The investigation had also exposed the deep flaws in the justice system. It was not a perfect machine, capable of delivering absolute justice, but a flawed human system susceptible to corruption, deceit, and manipulation. He had seen firsthand how those with power could use it to cover up their crimes, to shield themselves from accountability, and to silence those who sought to expose them.

John found himself questioning the very essence of justice. Was it truly attainable? Was it merely a facade, a hollow promise? He had spent years seeking it, driven by a sense of duty and a profound love for his sister. But the truth, he realized, was often messy, filled with shades of gray and ambiguous answers.

He had confronted Peter, the man who had orchestrated Sarah's disappearance, the man who had concealed his crimes for years, who had lived a life of privilege and deception while Sarah's memory was shrouded in mystery. He had brought Peter to justice, but the weight of his sister's loss remained.

He had also confronted David, the man who had been framed for Sarah's disappearance, the man who had been caught in the crosshairs of Peter's machinations. He had released David from a prison of false accusations, but he knew that David's life had been forever altered by the events of the investigation.

The scars of the past, both personal and societal, were deeply etched into John's soul. He carried the weight of Sarah's loss, the knowledge of Peter's deceit, and the realization that the pursuit of justice could be a long and arduous journey. He knew that he would never fully recover from the trauma of his sister's disappearance, that the memories would always linger, a constant reminder of the fragility of life and the enduring power of grief.

He found himself seeking solace in the company of those who loved him, those who had stood by him throughout his journey. His family, his friends, offered him a sense of comfort and support, a reminder that he was not alone in his struggle. They reminded him of the importance of love, compassion, and forgiveness, even in the face of profound loss.

He had to find a way to forgive, not for the sake of Peter or David, but for his own sake. He had to find a way to release himself from the anger and bitterness that had consumed him, to let go of the need for revenge, to embrace a path of healing and reconciliation.

John realized that the aftermath of the investigation was not a finish line but a new beginning. He had to find a way to move forward, to find meaning and purpose in the face of adversity. He had to find a way to honor Sarah's memory, not by dwelling on her loss, but by embracing life with renewed purpose, by finding ways to make a difference in the world, by seeking to create a more just and equitable society.

He understood that the pursuit of justice was a lifelong endeavor, a journey that never truly ended. He was not seeking to avenge his sister's death, but to prevent others from suffering the same fate. He was seeking to create a world where truth and justice prevailed, a world where the secrets of the past were not buried but exposed, a world where the vulnerable were protected and the powerful held accountable.

John's journey had left him with a profound sense of purpose, a renewed commitment to seeking justice, and a deep appreciation for the fragility of life. He had learned that the fight for truth and justice was an ongoing battle, one that demanded courage, perseverance, and an unwavering commitment to what was right. He knew that the scars of the past would always remain, but he was determined to move forward, to embrace the challenges of the present, and to find hope for a better future.

The weight of the truth settled on John like a leaden cloak. He had found his sister's killer, but the ache in his heart refused to abate. The years he'd spent consumed by the mystery, the nights haunted by Sarah's absence, the relentless pursuit of justice – it all seemed to culminate in a hollow victory. Justice, he realized, could never truly bring back what had been stolen. Sarah's laughter, their childhood adventures, the shared dreams they'd woven together – these were forever lost, a tapestry ripped apart by a cruel twist of fate.

The revelation of Peter's guilt had been a blow, not just for John but for the entire family. The shock, the disbelief, the anger – these emotions churned within them, leaving a trail of devastation. The man they had known, the seemingly harmless neighbor, had been a predator lurking in the shadows, a wolf in sheep's clothing.

John couldn't shake the feeling that something wasn't quite right, an uneasiness that lingered despite the closure of the case. He had spent years grappling with the loss of his sister, the burden of her unsolved disappearance weighing heavily on his mind. Finding her killer had brought a sense of relief, a finality to the agonizing quest. But now, the weight of her death, the cruel reality of what had happened to her, settled upon him like a thick fog.

He found himself revisiting the past, each memory a sharp shard of pain. Sarah's laughter echoed in his mind, her bright smile a painful reminder of what was gone. He saw her face in the family photographs, a constant reminder of the stolen years, the countless moments they could have shared.

John retreated into himself, the silence of his apartment a sanctuary from the cacophony of grief. He sought solace in the familiar routine of his work, the rhythm of his daily tasks providing a semblance of order amidst the chaos within.

He knew that time wouldn't heal the wounds, but he hoped it would soften their edges. He clung to the hope that one day, he would find a semblance of peace, a way to live with the pain, the memories a bittersweet reminder of the love they had shared.

The investigation had left scars, deep and indelible. The memories of the crime scene, the chilling details of Sarah's final moments, the relentless pursuit of the truth

– these were etched into his mind, an unwelcome companion. He couldn't escape them, the past a constant presence, a ghost whispering in the shadows.

The revelation of the secret society had been a shocking twist, a layer of darkness beneath the surface of the seemingly ordinary. The knowledge that such a corrupt and powerful organization could operate undetected, manipulating the lives of innocent people, was a chilling realization. The fight for justice was no longer a solitary endeavor but a battle against a formidable enemy.

John felt a deep sense of responsibility, a weight of purpose that he hadn't anticipated. He knew that exposing the society's crimes would put him in danger, but he couldn't turn away. His sister's memory, the countless victims of this corrupt system, demanded justice. He had to expose the truth, to fight for a world where justice prevailed.

But the path ahead was fraught with uncertainties. He had no way of knowing what lay ahead, the potential risks and consequences looming large. The secret society was a formidable opponent, a hydra with many heads, their reach extending far beyond the confines of this case.

The burden of loss, the weight of the truth, the ever-present fear – all of this weighed heavily upon John. But he knew that he couldn't give up. His sister's memory demanded that he continue the fight, to honor her life by seeking justice, to fight for a better world, a world where the innocent were protected and the truth prevailed. He knew that the journey ahead would be long and arduous, filled with danger and uncertainty. But he was determined to see it through, to fight for his sister, to fight for justice.

The air hung heavy in the small, sterile room. The scent of antiseptic and despair clung to John's senses, mingling with the faint, metallic tang of blood. The weight of the past, the unbearable weight of his sister's disappearance, pressed down on him like a physical force, a constant, throbbing ache in his chest.

He had spent the past few weeks revisiting the memories, the agonizing details of Sarah's last days, replaying them like a broken record in his mind. Each time, he hoped for some new revelation, a missing piece that would unravel the mystery, but he was left with the same crushing emptiness. He saw her again, young and vibrant, her laughter echoing in his ears, a ghost of the life that had been stolen from her. He could almost feel her presence, a phantom limb, a gaping hole in his life.

The investigation, the painstaking process of piecing together the fragments of Sarah's life, had been a grueling journey, filled with dead ends, false leads, and the constant sting of disappointment. The truth, when it finally emerged, had been a double-edged sword. It had brought closure, a semblance of justice, but it had also brought a new layer of pain, a visceral awareness of the depths of human depravity.

He had thought that finding the killer would provide

some solace, a sense of completion, but the reality was far more complicated. It had been a long, twisted road, filled with harrowing discoveries and agonizing confrontations. The investigation had unearthed a web of secrets and lies, revealing the darkness that lurked beneath the surface of their seemingly ordinary lives. He had been forced to confront the reality that the killer had been living among them all along, a familiar face hidden in plain sight.

The revelation of Peter's involvement had been a shock, a gut punch that left him reeling. It had shattered the illusion of a safe and stable world, forcing him to acknowledge the vulnerability of their existence. The knowledge that his sister's life had been taken by someone he had known, someone who had shared his life, was a heavy burden to bear.

John found himself struggling to reconcile the image of the seemingly ordinary man he had known with the cold, calculating killer who had taken Sarah's life. The realization that Peter had been capable of such brutality, that he had manipulated those around him for his own gain, left him feeling betrayed and violated. It was a betrayal not only of Sarah but of everyone who had known Peter, a stark reminder of the deceptive nature of appearances.

He had been forced to confront the darker aspects of himself, the anger, the resentment, the overwhelming need for vengeance. The investigation had brought out the worst in him, pushing him to the edge of his sanity.

But it had also forced him to confront his own vulnerabilities, his own capacity for pain and despair.

He had learned the importance of resilience, the power of forgiveness, and the enduring strength of human connection. He had witnessed the depths of human darkness, but he had also seen the extraordinary capacity for compassion and love. He had discovered the power of truth, the importance of standing up for what is right, even when the odds are stacked against him.

He was left with a profound sense of loss, but also a glimmer of hope. He carried the memory of his sister with him, knowing that her life had been cut short, but also knowing that her spirit would continue to inspire him. He found solace in the love and support of his family and friends, those who had stood by him through the darkness, those who had helped him to find his way back to the light.

The investigation had been a crucible, a harrowing journey that had tested him to his limits. But it had also been a profound journey of self-discovery, a process of growth and healing. He had learned to live with the scars of the past, acknowledging the pain and loss, but also embracing the resilience and hope that had helped him to survive.

The world had tilted on its axis. The ground beneath John's feet felt unsteady, the familiar contours of his life now warped and unfamiliar. The revelation of Peter's crimes had shattered a fragile peace, replacing it with a wave of grief and exhaustion that threatened to drown him. He had brought his sister's killer to justice, but the victory tasted like ashes in his mouth. The knowledge that her death had been a cold, calculated act, orchestrated by someone he had known for years, gnawed at him with a relentless ferocity.

He felt a hollowness within him, a void left by the stolen years, the laughter, the shared memories, the dreams they had once held. The weight of her absence was a constant companion, a heavy cloak he could not shake off. He understood that no amount of justice, no courtroom victory, could ever fill that void. He was left with the stark reality of his loss, a relentless ache that echoed through his being. He had brought her killer to justice, but what was the point of that justice if it couldn't bring her back?

The world around him was a cacophony of sound, yet all John could hear was the echo of her laughter, the gentle lilt of her voice. He could almost feel her presence, see her smile, but it was just a fleeting phantom, a cruel echo of what was lost. The pain was sharp and raw, a constant reminder of the life that was no more. It was a pain that resonated not just in his heart, but in the very fabric of his being, a wound that defied the passage of time.

He sought solace in the embrace of his family, his friends, seeking a haven from the storm that raged within him. They offered words of comfort, tears of sympathy, but he felt an insurmountable distance between their grief and his own. Their pain was palpable, their sorrow genuine, but their loss was different. They had shared years with Sarah, memories that were vivid and tangible, whereas John was left with fragments, fleeting moments captured in the lens of time.

The familiar routines of his life felt hollow, devoid of meaning. His work, once a source of purpose, now felt like a meaningless exercise. The pursuit of justice, the relentless chase of truth, had consumed him, but now it felt like a hollow shell, a monument to a loss that could not be filled. He was adrift in a sea of grief, lost in the currents of his own sorrow.

He knew that the process of healing was not a linear journey, but a series of fits and starts, a constant ebb and flow of emotions. There were moments of clarity, glimmers of hope, when he felt the weight of grief lifting, only to be swallowed whole by a new wave of sorrow. It was a process he had to navigate, a terrain he had to explore, step by painful step.

John sought solace in the quiet moments, the quiet corners of his life. He would sit by the window, watching the world go by, letting the sun warm his face, and he would try to find peace in the stillness. He would close his eyes and picture Sarah, her laughter echoing in his mind, her smile warming his heart. He would try to remember the good times, the moments of joy, the love they had shared.

But even in those quiet moments, the pain would return, a sharp pang of loss that would leave him gasping for breath. He would fight back tears, willing himself to be strong, but the pain would overwhelm him. It was a cycle he could not escape, a relentless reminder of the life that had been stolen from him.

The process of healing was a slow one. It was a journey of acceptance, a recognition of the pain, and a willingness to let go of the anger, the resentment, the bitterness. It was a journey of learning to live with the loss, of finding a new normal, a way to embrace the memories without being consumed by them.

He found solace in the small things, the simple joys that life offered. He would spend time with his family, sharing stories, creating new memories. He would go for walks, taking in the beauty of the world around him. He would listen to music, letting the melodies soothe his soul.

He knew that the pain would never truly go away, but he also knew that he could learn to live with it. He could find a way to honor Sarah's memory, to carry her spirit with him, to keep her alive in his heart. It would be a lifelong journey, a constant process of growth and acceptance, but it was a journey he was willing to take.

As John sat by the window, watching the sun set, he saw a glimmer of hope in the distance. The sky was ablaze with color, a kaleidoscope of orange and red, a promise of a new beginning. He knew that he would never fully recover from the loss of his sister, but he also knew that he could find a way to live a life that was filled with purpose and meaning. He would carry her memory with him always, but he would also embrace the future, knowing that Sarah would want him to be happy. She would want him to live a life that was full of love and laughter, a life that was worthy of her memory.

John stood before Sarah's grave, the weight of the past heavy upon his shoulders. The crisp autumn air carried the scent of fallen leaves, a bittersweet reminder of the seasons that had passed since his sister's disappearance. He had found the man responsible, but the pain of her absence still lingered, a hollow ache that no amount of justice could fully heal.

The investigation had been a grueling odyssey, a journey that had taken him through the darkest corners of his family's past and into the hidden crevices of his own heart. He had faced betrayal, deceit, and a chilling revelation that had shaken his very core - the truth about David and his involvement in Sarah's disappearance. But as he stood before her grave, a quiet sense of peace settled upon him. He had brought justice to his sister's memory, and that was all that mattered.

The weight of truth had been immense, crushing him under the realization that his sister's killer had lived among them, a seemingly ordinary man hiding a sinister secret. The investigation had forced him to confront his own vulnerabilities, to acknowledge the scars that the past had etched upon his soul. He had learned the importance of perseverance, the value of truth, even when it was painful, and the power of human connection in navigating through adversity.

The road to healing was not a linear path. It was a winding, treacherous journey through a landscape of grief, anger, and despair. John had sought solace in the memories of his sister, embracing the moments of joy and laughter that had filled their childhood. He had found strength in the unwavering support of his family and friends, their love a guiding light in the darkness.

His relationship with his family had been transformed. The shared grief had forged a deeper bond, a shared understanding of the pain that loss could inflict. He realized that their connection had been tested but had emerged stronger, a testament to the enduring power of family.

John had learned to embrace the complexities of grief, accepting that healing was a journey, not a destination. He understood that the pain of his sister's loss would always remain, a silent companion that would walk beside him through life. But he had also learned to find peace in the memories of his sister, to cherish the moments they had shared, and to honor her legacy by living a life that reflected the love and compassion she had embodied.

The investigation had irrevocably changed him. He was no longer the same man who had entered the police station 25 years ago, driven by a need to find answers. He had emerged from the crucible of his ordeal with a newfound sense of purpose, a determination to seek justice for those who had been wronged, and a belief in the enduring power of truth.

He knew that the shadows of the past would always linger, but he also knew that he had the strength to navigate those shadows. He had found resilience in the face of adversity, a strength that had been forged through the crucible of grief and loss.

As he gazed at the tombstone, a simple inscription bearing his sister's name, a profound sense of gratitude washed over him. He had found closure, not in the sense of forgetting, but in the acceptance of the truth and the understanding that he had done everything in his power to honor his sister's memory.

He left the cemetery with a heavy heart, but also with a newfound sense of purpose. The world was still a dangerous place, but he was no longer the same man. He had faced his demons and emerged stronger, carrying the spirit of his sister within him, a constant reminder of the importance of truth, justice, and the unyielding power of love.

Chapter 9: The Last Photographs

The vintage camera, a silent witness to Sarah's final moments, sat on the table before him, the worn leather cool against his fingertips. The faded photographs inside, each one a precious fragment of his sister's life, had become his obsession. He had meticulously examined every detail, every shadow, every fleeting expression captured within those fragile frames. The camera had been Sarah's, a gift from their father for her 18th birthday, and it held more than just images; it held memories, secrets, and the echoes of a life abruptly cut short.

John had been a detective for 25 years, and he had seen his fair share of horrors, but nothing had ever prepared him for the relentless ache that consumed him since Sarah's disappearance. He had dedicated himself to finding her, to bringing her killer to justice, but his pursuit had led him down a labyrinth of dead ends and shattered hopes. He had spent years chasing shadows, piecing together fragmented clues, only to have them vanish into thin air.

The blurry photograph, the only concrete lead he had, had been a cruel tease. The image of Sarah's fleeting smile, frozen in time, was marred by a shadowy figure looming behind her, a specter of death that had haunted his dreams ever since. He had identified the figure as Michael, a family friend who had been suspiciously absent on the day Sarah disappeared, but the evidence against him had been circumstantial. The case had gone cold, but John had never given up hope.

Now, as he held the camera again, a renewed sense of purpose surged through him. There was something about the photographs, something he had missed before. It was subtle, almost imperceptible, a faint shift in the light, a subtle anomaly that drew his attention. The photographs were not just images of Sarah, they were messages. He had spent years seeking answers in the blurry photograph, but the answer had been hidden in plain sight, waiting for him to see.

He studied the pictures, each one a snapshot of a life that had once been filled with joy and laughter. There was a photo of Sarah at the beach, her hair flying in the wind, her eyes sparkling with youthful exuberance. Then there was a picture of her in her childhood bedroom, surrounded by toys and trinkets, her face a mix of innocence and mischief.

He noticed that in each photograph, Sarah had subtly positioned a small object, a piece of jewelry, a book, a flower, each one carefully chosen, each one a tiny clue to a secret she had kept hidden from her family. He had spent years trying to understand Sarah, to unravel the mystery of her disappearance, but he had never considered that she might have been keeping a part of herself hidden.

The camera had become a bridge to Sarah, a way to connect with her even after her death. The photographs were more than just images; they were her voice, her legacy. He had always believed that Sarah had been a happy, well-adjusted young woman, but the photographs told a different story. They revealed a depth of emotion, a sense of longing, and a longing for connection that had been hidden beneath the surface.

John felt a surge of guilt, realizing that he had never truly understood his sister. He had been so focused on finding her killer, on seeking justice for her death, that he had forgotten to simply listen to her, to understand the woman she had become.

He had been too busy chasing shadows to see the light that shone through the cracks in his sister's carefully constructed facade. He had been so focused on the mystery of her disappearance that he had missed the mystery of her life.

As John examined the photographs, he felt a growing sense of urgency. The clues Sarah had left behind were not just a message, they were a desperate plea, a last attempt to connect with him before her fate was sealed. He had to understand her secrets, her fears, her hopes. He had to know why she had felt the need to hide a part of herself from him.

John was determined to unravel the mystery of Sarah's life, to understand the secrets she had kept hidden, and to finally find peace in the aftermath of her disappearance. He knew that the answers he was seeking might be painful, might challenge his perception of his sister, but he was willing to face the truth, no matter how difficult it might be.

He knew that his sister's secrets had been carefully guarded, hidden behind a veil of smiles and laughter. But he was determined to find her voice, to hear her story, and to honor her memory by finally understanding the woman she had become. The vintage camera, a symbol of his sister's life and her untimely death, had become a gateway to the truth. The photographs were not just memories; they were a map to the secrets of her heart, a map that he was determined to follow.

The photographs, each a silent snapshot of Sarah's final days, held a strange power over John. They were like whispers from the past, carrying echoes of her laughter, her anxieties, and the unspoken secrets she had carried. He saw her at a local cafe, her hand resting on a worn journal, her brow furrowed in concentration. He saw her in a park, her eyes filled with a distant longing, a look that spoke of a yearning for something just out of reach. He saw her at a library, her face illuminated by the soft glow of a lamp, a book clasped in her hand, a faint smile playing on her lips.

These glimpses, though fleeting, offered a glimpse into Sarah's inner world, a world that had always remained closed to him. He recognized the journal, a worn leather-bound book with a simple silver clasp, one she often carried with her. He remembered how she would disappear into her room, a book in her hand, her face lost in thought, her pen scratching furiously on paper. He knew that she wrote in this journal, pouring her heart out onto the pages, sharing her deepest thoughts and fears. He had always assumed it was a diary, a repository of teenage angst and daydreams. But now, as he held the photographs in his hand, he knew there was something more, something deeper, something she had kept hidden from everyone.

Driven by a desperate need to understand his sister, a desire to bridge the gap between them, John set out to find this journal. The photographs, with their cryptic clues, led him on a winding path through the city, past familiar landmarks, hidden alleyways, and forgotten corners. He retraced Sarah's steps, following the trail left behind by her ghost, a trail that led him to a small bookstore nestled on a quiet side street, a place she often visited, a place where she found solace and inspiration.

He entered the bookstore, the scent of old paper and ink filling his senses, the quiet hum of the city a distant murmur. He saw the same worn leather-bound journal on display, its pages waiting to be filled with stories untold. He knew this was the key, the gateway to his sister's secrets. He carefully examined the journal, the faded cover, the worn pages, each marking a testament to its owner's deep connection with it. He wondered what secrets lay hidden within its pages, what stories she had kept locked away, what truths she had chosen to bury. He carefully lifted the journal from its display, its weight surprisingly familiar in his hands, as if he had held it countless times before. He flipped through the pages, the scent of aging paper and ink filling his nostrils. The ink, faded with time, spoke of emotions long buried, of dreams once held, of fears once faced.

He was careful not to tear the pages, each one precious, each one a fragment of his sister's soul. He read her words, her thoughts, her hopes, and her fears, feeling a profound connection to her, a connection that had been lost for so long. He saw her struggles, her triumphs, her vulnerabilities, and her strength. He learned about her loves, her losses, her secrets, and her dreams. He discovered that Sarah had been grappling with a personal secret, a truth that she had never revealed to her family.

As he read, the words seemed to come alive, painting a vivid picture of his sister's life, her heart laid bare, her soul exposed. He saw the pain she had endured, the betrayals she had suffered, the loneliness she had carried. He felt her anguish, her despair, her longing for connection. He was drawn into her world, a world of unspoken desires, hidden emotions, and unfulfilled dreams.

He read about a love she had kept secret, a love that had burned fiercely, then faded into the ashes of betrayal. He read about a man, a man who had captivated her heart, promised her the world, then shattered her dreams. He saw the vulnerability, the heartbreak, the scars that love had left behind. He saw the fear, the doubt, the shame that she had carried within her, a secret she had hidden for years. He understood why she had kept a distance from her family, why she had been so secretive about her life. He realized that she had been trying to protect them, to shield them from the pain she had endured, the scars she had carried. He saw her courage, her strength, her resilience, her unwavering desire to protect the ones she loved.

As he read, he felt a surge of empathy, a deep understanding of the pain his sister had suffered. He realized that he had never truly known her, that he had only seen the surface, the facade she had presented to the world. He felt a wave of sorrow, a sense of loss, a realization that he had missed out on so much. He wished he had been there for her, that he had been able to share her burdens, to ease her pain. He wished he had been able to understand her, to see the world through her eyes. He wished he could have told her how much he loved her, how much he had always cared.

But now, as he held the journal in his hands, he felt a sense of connection, a sense of understanding, a sense of peace. He felt as if he had finally begun to understand his sister, to see the world through her eyes. He felt a sense of closure, a sense of acceptance, a sense of love. He realized that even though she was gone, her spirit lived on in his heart, in his memories, in the words he had read. He knew that he would never forget her, that her memory would always be a part of him. He vowed to honor her memory, to carry her spirit with him always, to live a life filled with love, compassion, and understanding. He would remember her as she was, a woman of strength, resilience, and grace, a woman who had carried a heavy burden but had never lost her spirit, her love, her hope.

John's discovery of Sarah's journal was a turning point in his journey, a journey that had taken him through darkness and despair, but had also led him to a place of understanding, acceptance, and love. The photographs had been his guide, leading him to a hidden truth, a truth that had been buried for years. The truth about his sister's life, her love, her loss, and her secrets. It was a truth that had changed him forever, a truth that had brought him closer to his sister, a truth that had taught him the importance of love, compassion, and understanding.

John traced the lines of the photograph with his fingertips, his heart heavy with a mixture of grief and a newfound understanding. The image, once a chilling glimpse into his sister's final moments, now held a different weight – a secret that had been buried for years, a truth that Sarah had kept hidden even from her own family. The photograph wasn't just a visual record of her last moments, it was a cryptic message, a coded plea that he had only just begun to decipher.

He had meticulously examined every detail of the photograph, every shadow, every blur. He had sought the advice of experts, forensic analysts, and photographers, hoping to glean any hidden information. He had pored over Sarah's personal belongings, searching for clues that would help him understand her life. But it was the photograph, the last one taken of his sister before her disappearance, that had finally provided the key.

The secret lay in the details, in the subtle angles, the positioning of the camera, the composition of the image. The photograph, taken from a slightly elevated angle, captured Sarah standing against a backdrop of trees. It seemed like an ordinary image, a casual snapshot taken during a leisurely walk. But John, fueled by his love for his sister and a desperate yearning for answers, saw something more. He saw a deliberate arrangement, a planned composition, a carefully crafted message.

He noticed a slight shift in the camera angle, a subtle tilt that wasn't accidental. He realized that the trees in the background were strategically positioned, their branches forming a kind of symbolic frame around Sarah. And finally, he saw the way she was holding her hands, a subtle gesture that he realized was a coded signal.

The secret that Sarah had kept hidden for years was a secret about her past, about a love she had kept hidden from her family, about a relationship that had left her heartbroken. It was a secret she had carried with her, a burden she had kept hidden, a truth she had feared to share.

The photographs led John to a secluded spot on the outskirts of town, a place that Sarah had visited often, a place that had held a special meaning for her. There, beneath the shade of an ancient oak tree, he found a small, wooden box buried beneath a layer of leaves. The box was old, worn, and slightly weathered, but it was still intact. Inside, he found a journal, Sarah's journal, filled with her thoughts, her dreams, and her secrets.

The journal was a window into Sarah's soul, a testament to her hidden life, a world that she had kept separate from her family. He read through her entries, his heart aching with empathy, his mind grappling with the complexity of his sister's life.

He learned about a young man named Mark, a man who had captured Sarah's heart, a man who had promised her the world. They had met at a summer camp, their connection instantaneous, their bond unbreakable. They had spent their days laughing, sharing secrets, and dreaming of a future together.

Mark had been charming, charismatic, and deeply in love with Sarah. But he had also been secretive, possessive, and ultimately, destructive. He had betrayed Sarah's trust, breaking her heart into a million pieces. He had left her feeling shattered, betrayed, and alone.

Sarah's entries in the journal revealed a woman who had been deeply wounded, a woman who had struggled to move on from the pain of Mark's betrayal. She had bottled up her emotions, keeping them hidden from her family, afraid to burden them with her pain. She had withdrawn from her loved ones, building a wall around her heart, afraid to let anyone in.

As John read through the journal entries, he realized that Sarah had kept her secret for a reason. She had feared her family's judgment, their disapproval, their disappointment. She had wanted to protect them from the pain of her heartbreak, to shield them from the truth of her shattered dreams. She had believed that her secret would be her burden alone.

John felt a surge of guilt and regret, realizing that he had been so focused on finding his sister's killer that he had neglected to truly understand her, to see the woman beneath the surface, to appreciate the strength and resilience that she had shown in the face of adversity. He had only known Sarah through the lens of his own grief, his own need for closure. He had never truly considered the complexities of her life, the hidden depths of her emotions, the unspoken burdens she had carried.

The journal revealed a different side of Sarah, a side that he had never known. It revealed a woman who had loved deeply, who had been betrayed, who had fought to rebuild her life, who had found strength in her vulnerability.

The journal's final entry, dated just days before her disappearance, spoke of a new beginning, a renewed sense of hope, a newfound strength. She wrote about a desire to reconnect with her family, to let them into her heart, to share her pain and her dreams. She wrote about her fear of the past, her fear of repeating the mistakes she had made, her fear of being hurt again.

John realized that Sarah's final entry in the journal held the key to her disappearance. She had been on the verge of breaking free, of revealing her secrets, of sharing her pain, of opening her heart. She had been ready to take back her life, to move on from the past.

But something had happened, something had stopped her. Something had silenced her.

As John closed the journal, his mind racing with questions, he realized that the real mystery wasn't just who had killed Sarah, but what had driven her to the point of secrecy, to the point of hiding her pain, to the point of being willing to bury her past.

The photograph, once a haunting reminder of his sister's disappearance, now held a different significance. It was a message from Sarah, a plea for understanding, a testament to the complexity of her life, a reminder of the secrets she had kept hidden.

And John, finally understanding the woman she had been, the pain she had endured, the secrets she had kept, was ready to embrace the truth of her life, to honor her memory, and to seek justice for the woman he had always loved.

John stood in Sarah's room, surrounded by her belongings. It had been untouched for years, a shrine to a life cut short. Dust motes danced in the afternoon sun, illuminating the faded photographs and trinkets that lined her shelves. He ran his fingers over the worn surface of her dresser, feeling the phantom weight of her presence.

It was in this room, amidst the remnants of her past, that he found the key to understanding Sarah's secret. It wasn't a hidden diary or a secret love letter, but a single, faded photograph. It was a picture of Sarah, taken in her early twenties, her smile as bright as the sun that had bleached the edges of the photo. She was holding a worn, leather-bound journal, its cover embossed with a delicate vine pattern. The journal was closed, but the way Sarah held it, her eyes gleaming with a mix of longing and sadness, told a story.

John knew the journal. He had seen it before, tucked away in a box of Sarah's old things. But back then, it had held no significance. Now, as he looked at the photograph, the image of Sarah's melancholic smile sparked a new understanding. He knew that his sister had been carrying a secret, a weight she had borne alone.

He went through Sarah's things, searching for the journal. It wasn't easy. Years had passed since he had last seen it, and the box was filled with countless mementos, each holding its own silent memories. But he persevered, driven by a need to understand his sister, to connect with the person she truly was.

Finally, he found it. The journal was tucked away in a small, velvet pouch, its pages worn and brittle with age. He carefully opened the cover, the leather creaking under his touch. The scent of old paper and faded ink filled his senses, taking him back to a time when Sarah was young and full of life.

The first page was blank. He turned to the next, his heart pounding with anticipation. The handwriting was delicate, flowing across the page with a graceful ease that was characteristic of Sarah. Her words were a journey into her soul, a tapestry woven with threads of joy, sorrow, and longing.

As he read through the journal, a world of secrets unfolded. He learned of a past relationship, a love that had burned bright but had ultimately left Sarah heartbroken. It was a story she had never shared with her family, a pain she had kept hidden, a burden she had carried alone.

He learned that Sarah had met a man named Thomas during her college years. They had fallen deeply in love, a love that had filled her with joy and hope for the future. But their love was not destined to last. Thomas had been a charming and charismatic man, but he was also deceitful and manipulative. He had broken Sarah's heart, leaving her shattered and disillusioned.

The journal chronicled Sarah's heartbreak, the pain of betrayal, and the struggle to pick up the pieces of her broken life. It was a testament to her strength and resilience, her ability to find hope in the face of adversity.

John read through Sarah's words, feeling a pang of sadness for the pain she had endured. He realized that he had never truly known his sister, the woman behind the smiles and the laughter. He had always seen her as a happy, carefree girl, but now he understood the depth of her emotions, the complexities of her life.

He felt a surge of anger towards Thomas, the man who had hurt his sister so deeply. But his anger was soon replaced by a profound sense of understanding. He knew that Sarah had chosen to keep this part of her life hidden from her family, to protect them from the pain she had endured. He understood that her decision had been born out of love and loyalty, a testament to her selfless nature.

He closed the journal, the weight of Sarah's secrets settling upon him. He understood that he would never truly know his sister, the woman she had become after that fateful encounter with Thomas. But he knew that her memory would always be a source of inspiration, a reminder of the power of love, the strength of resilience, and the importance of understanding.

He knew that his sister would have wanted him to move on, to find happiness in his own life. He vowed to honor her memory by embracing the complexities of life, by seeking understanding, and by cherishing the connections that brought him joy. He knew that his sister would have wanted him to live a life filled with love, laughter, and hope, a life that would be a testament to the enduring power of the human spirit.

John stood in his sister's room, surrounded by the remnants of her life. He'd spent the last few weeks sifting through her belongings, trying to piece together a picture of the woman she'd been. But Sarah had been a master at keeping secrets, and now, with her gone, John realized how little he truly knew her.

He held the vintage camera, the same one that had led him to the discovery of her remains. The camera, a silent witness to her final moments, had become a symbol of the truth he had finally unearthed. The photographs, blurry and grainy, had offered a glimpse into Sarah's last days, but they had also hinted at a hidden life, a world that Sarah had kept to herself.

He pulled out the journal he had found hidden within Sarah's belongings, a small leather-bound volume tucked away in a secret compartment of her dresser. The pages were filled with Sarah's handwriting, a collection of her innermost thoughts and feelings, her hopes and dreams, her struggles and triumphs.

As John read through Sarah's journal entries, he felt a wave of sadness wash over him. Sarah had been carrying a heavy burden, a secret that she had kept hidden to protect her family. The man she had loved, the man she had thought would be her forever, had betrayed her, leaving her heartbroken and shattered. John had never known about this, and the knowledge of Sarah's pain, the pain she had kept hidden for so long, made him ache for her.

Sarah had written about a man named Peter, a man who had promised her the world but had ultimately shattered her dreams. She had described their passionate romance, the intensity of their feelings, and the devastating betrayal that had ripped their world apart. Sarah had been left broken, her faith in love shattered, and she had never been able to fully recover.

The more John read, the more he realized how little he had known about his sister. Sarah had always been the quiet one, the one who kept to herself. She had been the observer, the one who watched from the sidelines, never revealing her own emotions or experiences. But now, through her journal entries, John saw a woman of depth and complexity, a woman who had been fighting her own battles, carrying her own burdens.

The realization that Sarah had never truly felt comfortable sharing her deepest secrets with her family filled him with a bittersweet mix of sadness and understanding. He saw now that she had kept her distance, not out of malice or indifference, but out of a deep need to protect herself, to protect them from the pain she was carrying.

The photos and journal entries had revealed a side of Sarah that John had never seen before. He saw a woman who had been deeply hurt, a woman who had been forced to navigate a world of pain and betrayal. But he also saw a woman who had been resilient, a woman who had found a way to survive, to keep going, even in the face of adversity.

John felt a surge of gratitude for Sarah's bravery, for her strength in the face of such heartbreak. He felt a profound sense of sorrow for her, for the pain she had carried, for the life she had been forced to live. He understood now that he never truly knew his sister, that she had been a mystery to him, even when they were together.

He resolved to honor her memory by embracing the complexities of her life, by understanding the person she truly was, even in her absence. He would cherish the memories of his sister, the precious moments they had shared, and he would learn from her lessons, carrying her spirit with him always.

Sarah's secret world, the world she had kept hidden from her family, had opened John's eyes to the profound depths of his sister's being. He realized that the pain she had carried had shaped her life, had shaped her into the woman she had become. He understood now that Sarah's pain had not defined her, but it had been a part of her, a part of her story, and he was determined to embrace that story, to honor her memory by carrying her spirit with him.

Chapter 10: The Shadows of the Past

The air in John's apartment was thick with the scent of stale coffee and the weight of unspoken grief. The once vibrant yellow walls felt dull and lifeless, a reflection of the emptiness that gnawed at his soul. He sat hunched over a worn photograph, his gaze fixated on the blurry image of his sister, Sarah, her face a ghostly apparition in the shadows. The camera, the sole survivor of her disappearance, held a secret that had haunted him for years.

The years since Sarah's disappearance had been a blur of agonizing memories and unanswered questions. John had poured his life into his work, hoping to find solace in the pursuit of justice for others. But the shadows of the past, the chilling reality of his sister's fate, followed him everywhere. The case had been declared cold, the evidence scant, the killer unknown. But John knew that somewhere out there, someone was responsible for his sister's disappearance, someone who had been living among them all along.

The image of the blurry photo had become an obsession. John had spent countless hours studying it, squinting at the details, searching for any clue that could lead him to Sarah's killer. The more he looked, the more the image seemed to shift and morph. The shadowy figure behind Sarah, a fleeting glimpse of the killer, was a constant torment. Was it a face he recognized? Could it be someone he knew? The question gnawed at his mind, driving him to the brink of madness.

Sleep offered no escape. The nightmares came in waves, vivid and terrifying, each one replaying the horror of that fateful day. He would see Sarah's terrified face, hear her desperate pleas for help. The shadowy figure would loom over him, his eyes piercing, his voice a chilling whisper. He would wake up drenched in sweat, his heart pounding, the room swirling with darkness.

His memories of Sarah were a bittersweet tapestry. He remembered her infectious laughter, her fiery spirit, her unwavering loyalty. He remembered the countless hours they spent together, playing in their backyard, sharing secrets, building a world of their own. He remembered the day she disappeared, the chilling silence that descended on their home, the fear that gripped his heart. He remembered the frantic search, the endless hope, the crushing disappointment.

John had never given up hope. The years had only fueled his determination to find answers. He had dedicated himself to his job, becoming a seasoned detective, a relentless pursuer of justice. But the weight of Sarah's case pressed down on him, a heavy burden that threatened to consume him. The memories of the investigation, the dead ends, the false leads, the agonizing realization that the killer could be someone he knew, haunted him.

He couldn't shake the feeling that he was missing something, that there was a piece of the puzzle he hadn't found. The blurry photo, with its ghostly image of Sarah and the elusive glimpse of the killer, became a symbol of the unsolved mystery, a reminder of the lingering questions that tormented him.

John knew he had to find closure, to bring justice to his sister's memory. He had to find the killer, to face the person who had taken Sarah from him, to unravel the truth that had been hidden for years. But as he delved deeper into the past, he began to realize that the truth might not be what he expected. He might have to confront the darkness within himself, the ghosts of his own memories, and the unsettling reality that the killer might be closer than he imagined.

The investigation had taken its toll. John was a shadow of his former self, his eyes haunted by the past, his spirit weary from the relentless pursuit of truth. But he couldn't give up. He had to find answers, not just for himself, but for Sarah. He had to find a way to escape the shadows that had haunted him for so long, to find a glimmer of peace in the midst of his pain. He knew that finding the truth wouldn't erase the pain, but it might help him to finally heal. He had to find a way to move forward, to find a way to live with the memories, to find a way to honor Sarah's legacy.

The silence in the apartment was deafening, broken only by the rhythmic ticking of the grandfather clock in the hallway. John sat in his worn armchair, the vintage camera clutched in his hand, its cold metal a stark contrast to the warmth of the worn leather beneath his fingers. The blurry photograph, the sole evidence of Sarah's final moments, seemed to stare back at him, a silent accusation, a cruel reminder of the past that refused to let go.

He had finally found his sister's killer. David, a man whose obsession with Sarah had spiraled into a terrifying reality, had confessed to his crimes, his words echoing in John's ears, a chilling testament to the darkness that lurked beneath a seemingly ordinary facade. The case was closed, justice had been served, but the weight of the truth felt heavier than ever.

John felt a wave of exhaustion wash over him, the culmination of months of tireless investigation, sleepless nights, and the emotional turmoil of confronting the truth about his sister's fate. He had sought solace in the resolution of the case, a sense of closure that had eluded him for years. Yet, as he sat there, the photograph clutched in his hand, a chilling truth seeped into his soul: closure didn't erase the pain, it merely shifted its form, leaving him grappling with a new set of questions, a different kind of torment.

He thought of the numerous faces he had encountered during the investigation: the grieving family, the weary detectives, the cunning suspects, each one a puzzle piece in the intricate mosaic of Sarah's disappearance. He had delved into their lives, their motivations, their secrets, seeking answers, seeking understanding, but the deeper he went, the more he realized the futility of his quest. He had found answers, but they had only raised more questions.

The nature of justice, the reliability of memory, the complexities of human nature - these were the questions that haunted him now, the shadows of the past that refused to recede. He had brought justice to Sarah, but what did that mean in the grand scheme of things? Did it truly erase the pain, the trauma, the lingering sense of injustice? Did it offer any solace for the family, for himself? Or was it merely a fleeting moment of satisfaction, a temporary reprieve from the overwhelming weight of loss?

He questioned the motives of the people involved, the choices they made, the paths they took that had led them to this point. He thought of Michael, the family friend, burdened by guilt and suspicion, his own memories of that fateful day blurred by time and doubt. Had Michael truly been innocent, a victim of circumstance, or had he played a role in Sarah's disappearance? The answer, he knew, would forever remain shrouded in the mists of time, a haunting uncertainty that would linger in his thoughts.

He thought of Emily, the childhood friend, harboring a resentment that had festered for years, her own secrets buried deep within her, her truth obscured by a veil of deceit. He had uncovered her connection to the crime, the evidence pointing to her involvement, yet he still couldn't shake off the feeling that he had only scratched the surface of her story. He wondered about her motivations, the extent of her involvement, and whether she was merely a pawn in a larger game, a player in a conspiracy that extended beyond the scope of his investigation.

He thought of David, the confessed killer, his obsession with Sarah revealing a chilling insight into the dark recesses of the human psyche. Yet, as he had delved deeper into David's life, John had found evidence that suggested a more complex narrative, a web of secrets and connections that hinted at a more sinister plot. Had David truly acted alone, or was he part of a larger conspiracy, a pawn in a game he didn't fully understand?

These questions, these doubts, these lingering shadows, they all coalesced into a single, overwhelming sense of unease. The investigation had brought a semblance of closure, a sense of justice served, but it had also unearthed a truth far more unsettling than he had imagined. It had revealed the fragility of human nature, the dark potential that lurked beneath the surface, and the enduring power of secrets to warp reality and twist perceptions.

John found himself wrestling with the weight of his own memories, the memories of Sarah, the memories of that fateful day, the memories of the investigation, all swirling together in a dizzying kaleidoscope of pain and uncertainty. He had sought answers, but the answers he had found were more like shadows, elusive, shifting, refusing to coalesce into a clear picture.

He was haunted by the notion that he had only scratched the surface of the truth, that there were still secrets to be uncovered, truths to be revealed. He felt an overwhelming sense of unfinished business, a need to delve deeper, to unravel the mysteries that lingered in the shadows. He was no longer seeking closure; he was seeking understanding, a grasp on the truth that eluded him, a way to make sense of the chaos that had engulfed his life.

The photograph lay in his hand, a stark reminder of Sarah's final moments, a window into the past that refused to be closed. It was a testament to the enduring power of secrets, the chilling reality that the truth could be hidden in plain sight, disguised by the fog of time and the complexities of human behavior. The past, he realized, was not a static entity but a fluid, ever-shifting landscape, a collection of memories that could be distorted, manipulated, and even fabricated.

John stood up, the camera still clutched in his hand, the weight of the photograph pressing against his palm. He walked towards the window, the city lights blurring into a kaleidoscope of color as he gazed out at the cityscape. The shadows of the past stretched long and dark, reaching out to engulf him, but he refused to succumb. He was a detective, a seeker of truth, and he would continue to chase the shadows until they were no more.

There are still questions that remain unanswered, mysteries that continue to linger in John's mind. He wonders about the true extent of Peter's involvement and whether there were other individuals who were complicit in Sarah's disappearance. He contemplates the possibility of a larger conspiracy, a network of individuals who had been operating in the shadows, pulling strings and influencing events for their own gain.

The unsettling truth is that even with Peter's confession, John is left with a sense of unease, a feeling that something is still missing. The pieces of the puzzle don't quite fit together, leaving him with a nagging suspicion that there is more to the story.

He revisits the events of the investigation, analyzing the evidence and the testimonies, searching for any inconsistencies or overlooked clues. He carefully examines the photographs from the vintage camera, hoping to find hidden messages or clues that might shed light on the unanswered questions. He scrutinizes the composite sketch of the killer, wondering if there are any subtle details that were missed, any slight discrepancies that could lead him to a different conclusion.

John's intuition tells him that he is not dealing with a simple case of a disgruntled ex-employee seeking revenge. The complexity of the events, the multiple layers of deceit and betrayal, suggest a deeper, more sinister motive at play. He realizes that the investigation has uncovered just the tip of the iceberg, a glimpse into a darker world of secrets and lies.

He contemplates the possibility that Peter was merely a pawn in a larger game, a willing participant in a scheme orchestrated by someone else. He wonders if there were others who had a stake in Sarah's disappearance, individuals who had benefited from her demise.

John's mind races as he considers the different possibilities, his suspicions growing with each passing day. He is determined to find answers, to unravel the mysteries that remain. He feels a responsibility to his sister's memory, a duty to ensure that justice is served, even if it means venturing into uncharted territory, confronting the shadows of the past and facing the unsettling truth.

He begins to question his own assumptions, the conclusions he had drawn based on the evidence. He realizes that the truth can be elusive, easily manipulated and distorted, especially when those involved are skilled in deception. He acknowledges the limitations of memory, the way in which it can be influenced by emotions and biases, creating a distorted perception of reality.

John's journey of discovery is far from over. He knows that the investigation has only scratched the surface of the truth. There are still layers of deception to be peeled back, secrets to be uncovered, and truths to be revealed. He is driven by an unyielding determination to find answers, to unravel the complex web of lies and deceit that has shrouded his sister's disappearance for so long.

He knows that the path ahead will be fraught with danger and uncertainty, but he is determined to see it through. He is fueled by a love for his sister, a fierce desire for justice, and an unwavering belief in the power of truth. He will not rest until he has found the answers he seeks, until the shadows of the past have been banished and the truth has been brought to light.

The unanswered questions gnaw at John's mind, refusing to let him rest. He is haunted by the haunting silence of the past, the whispers of secrets yet to be revealed. He knows that the truth is out there, hidden somewhere within the labyrinth of events, waiting to be uncovered.

He is determined to delve deeper, to push beyond the limits of his investigation, to uncover the secrets that lie beneath the surface. He is committed to finding answers, to bringing justice to his sister's memory, and to exposing the truth, no matter the cost.

John's quest for understanding is a personal one, fueled by a profound need to make sense of the world and the people in it. He recognizes that the pursuit of justice is not merely about finding the guilty party, but about understanding the complexities of human nature, the motivations behind their actions, and the consequences of their choices.

He is driven by a desire to confront the darkness within himself, the fear and anger that have haunted him since his sister's disappearance. He recognizes that the journey of healing is not a linear one, but a process of constant growth and self-discovery, a journey that requires facing the uncomfortable truths about himself and the world around him.

John understands that the shadows of the past are long and deep, that they can cast a dark cloud over even the brightest of days. He is determined to confront these shadows, to shine a light on the darkness, and to find peace within himself. He is determined to find meaning and purpose in the face of adversity, to honor the memory of his sister, and to create a world where truth and justice prevail.

The quest for understanding is an ongoing one, a journey that will continue long after the investigation has concluded. John knows that he will always carry the weight of his sister's disappearance, but he is determined to find a way to live with it, to find peace in the midst of pain. He is committed to using his experience to help others, to fight for justice, and to create a world where truth and compassion prevail.

John sat in his dimly lit apartment, the silence broken only by the rhythmic ticking of the grandfather clock in the corner. The air was thick with the scent of stale coffee and regret. His hands, calloused and scarred from years of wrestling with truth and deception, held a worn photo – the one that had ignited his desperate search for answers. It was a blurry image, a ghostly testament to Sarah's final moments, capturing the fleeting glimpse of the killer that had haunted his dreams for decades. The image, a faded glimpse of a shadowy figure lurking behind his sister, had become his obsession, his reason for being. He couldn't let go, not until he had brought Sarah's killer to justice.

He had finally found closure, or so he thought. He had unmasked Peter, the man who had orchestrated Sarah's disappearance, the man who had lived among them, his true nature concealed beneath a facade of respectability. He had brought Peter down, dismantling his intricate web of lies and deceit, exposing his crimes to the world. But as the dust settled, as the headlines faded and the news cycle moved on, John found himself grappling with a chilling realization – the truth was more complex, more insidious than he had ever imagined.

He had brought Peter to justice, yes, but he couldn't shake the feeling that there were still shadows lurking in the corners of his mind, secrets whispering in the silence. He was haunted by unanswered questions, by the lingering feeling that he had only scratched the surface of a deeper, darker truth. He had exposed Peter, but who had pulled the strings from the shadows, orchestrating events from behind the scenes? Who had manipulated the lives of innocent people, using their pain and suffering as pawns in a twisted game of power?

The weight of these unanswered questions pressed down on him, a heavy burden that threatened to consume him. He couldn't bring himself to let go, not yet. There was still unfinished business, a lingering sense that the truth was out there, just beyond his grasp. He couldn't rest, not until he had unearthed the hidden truth, not until he had brought the perpetrators to justice, not until he had finally found a measure of peace.

He began by revisiting the evidence, every detail, every clue, examining them with fresh eyes, seeking patterns and connections that he had missed before. He poured over the photographs, the old newspaper articles, the witness statements, and the financial records, searching for a thread, a single clue that might unravel the tangled web of deception. He looked for the missing pieces, the pieces that would unlock the secrets hidden in the shadows.

His investigation led him to the remnants of a long-forgotten family feud, a bitter rivalry between the Sniders and the Peters that had spanned generations. He discovered that his family and Peter's family had been locked in a silent war, a constant battle for power and control. The feud, he realized, was not just a petty squabble; it was a tapestry woven with threads of greed, ambition, and revenge, a tapestry that had reached far beyond the confines of their small town. He began to see Sarah's disappearance in a new light, a chilling reminder that the battle had extended beyond their family, reaching into the heart of the town, leaving a trail of pain and devastation in its wake.

As John delved deeper, he found himself questioning the motives of those he thought he knew. He began to suspect that his own family, his closest allies, might be hiding secrets, their loyalty tested by the allure of power and the allure of the shadows. He had always believed that family was a sanctuary, a place of unconditional love and support, but the truth, he realized, was more complicated, more treacherous. The darkness, he discovered, could seep into the most intimate corners of life, corrupting those he held dear, leaving him questioning everything he had ever known.

He stumbled upon a hidden archive, a dusty repository of forgotten documents, buried deep within the heart of the town. He discovered a collection of files, meticulously compiled, that contained the records of a secret society, a clandestine organization that operated in the shadows, manipulating events and influencing lives from behind the scenes. The documents revealed a web of corruption and greed, a chilling reminder that power could be corrupted, its seductive allure twisting morality and twisting lives.

He learned that Sarah had stumbled upon the society's activities, her curiosity leading her to a truth she wasn't meant to see. She had threatened to expose their crimes, her determination to stand up for what was right a deadly threat to their power. Their response, he realized, had been swift and brutal, their control ironclad, their reach long and insidious.

John was consumed by a burning desire to uncover the truth, to expose the secrets of the secret society and bring their crimes to light. He knew the risks involved, the dangers of battling a shadowy organization that had operated with impunity for generations. He understood that his life, his very existence, might be at stake, but he couldn't stand by and watch as the shadows consumed the world around him.

He knew he couldn't fight them alone. He had to find others who had been targeted by the society, others who had been caught in their web of deception, others who were willing to stand up and fight for truth and justice. He reached out, using his connections, his intuition, and his growing understanding of the society's methods to connect with those who had been silenced, those who had been forced into hiding, those who had been betrayed. He was searching for allies, for kindred spirits, for those who understood the power of darkness and the strength it took to fight back.

He gathered his allies, a motley crew of individuals from all walks of life, each with their own story of loss and betrayal, each with their own reason to fight. He found a former journalist, ostracized for his investigative work, his career destroyed by the society's reach. He found a former lawyer, disillusioned by the corruption he had witnessed, his faith in the law shattered. He found a former government official, a whistleblower who had been silenced, his life threatened by the society's agents.

Together, they formed a united front, their shared experiences binding them together, their shared desire for justice driving them forward. They knew the risks, the dangers, but they were determined to expose the truth, no matter the cost. They understood that they were up against a powerful adversary, but they also understood the power of unity, the strength of their shared purpose. They were fighting for a better future, a future where the shadows could no longer hold sway.

They embarked on a perilous journey, navigating a treacherous path of secrets and lies, their lives hanging in the balance. They gathered evidence, piecing together fragments of a complex puzzle, tracing the society's reach through its intricate network of corruption. They exposed their crimes, bringing their secrets to light, exposing their manipulations and their betrayals. They fought back against their threats, their intimidation, their attempts to silence them. They were determined to bring down the society, to dismantle their empire of lies and greed.

Their efforts, however, were met with fierce resistance. The society's agents, shadowy figures who moved with a chilling efficiency, sought to neutralize them, to silence their voices, to crush their hope. John, his once-familiar world now a landscape of fear and paranoia, found himself constantly on edge, his instincts honed, his senses heightened. He was fighting for his life, for the lives of his allies, for the lives of everyone who had been touched by the society's corrupting influence.

The stakes were high, the dangers real, but John and his allies pressed on, their determination unwavering. They knew the truth was out there, just beyond their reach, and they were determined to find it, to bring it to light, to expose the darkness that had consumed so many lives. They were fighting for justice, for truth, for a future where the shadows could no longer hold sway.

John found himself adrift in a sea of memories, each wave washing over him with the force of a tidal surge. The weight of his sister's disappearance, the agony of her absence, and the years spent searching for answers had left an indelible mark. The investigation had unearthed the truth, but the truth itself was a tangled web of lies and deception, leaving more questions than answers. He was haunted by the shadows of the past, each one whispering doubts and fears that he struggled to silence.

He had finally unmasked the killer, Peter, but the man's confession had only opened a Pandora's box of new questions. The revelations of a secret society manipulating events from the shadows, their insidious influence reaching into every corner of society, had left him reeling. He had uncovered a conspiracy so deep, so pervasive, that it made him question everything he thought he knew about the world.

He had confronted the horrors of his sister's death, the realization that the person who had taken her from him had been lurking in the shadows, a hidden threat in their midst. He had tasted the bitter truth of betrayal, the realization that even those closest to him could harbor secrets and darkness. The investigation had torn away the façade of normalcy, revealing the stark reality of a world rife with hidden agendas and unspoken truths.

The scars of his journey were etched deep within him, a testament to the price of seeking justice. He carried the weight of the past on his shoulders, a constant reminder of the fragility of life, the capricious nature of fate, and the enduring power of darkness. The quest for answers had consumed him, leaving him drained and battered, but also empowered with a newfound resolve.

His journey had taken him to the darkest corners of his soul, forcing him to confront his own vulnerabilities and the depths of human depravity. He had grappled with the weight of guilt and the torment of unanswered questions. He had confronted the specter of his own mortality, realizing that life is a fragile thing, a fleeting moment in the grand tapestry of time.

He had sought solace in the memories of his sister, cherishing the moments they had shared, remembering her laughter and her light. He had found strength in the love and support of his family and friends, their unwavering belief in him a beacon of hope in the face of despair.

But the shadows of the past continued to linger, a constant reminder of the wounds that ran deep. He could not erase the images of his sister's disappearance, the pain of her absence, the unanswered questions that continued to torment him. He yearned for closure, for a sense of peace that would finally free him from the chains of the past.

John knew that the journey of healing was a long and arduous one, a process of confronting the darkness within and finding the light to guide him forward. He knew that the scars of the past would never fully fade, but he was determined to find a way to live with them, to carry their weight without succumbing to their grip.

He looked at the vintage camera, the lens reflecting the light of the setting sun, a haunting reminder of the photographs that had ignited his quest. He knew that the camera was more than just a tool, more than just a relic of the past. It was a symbol of his journey, of the truth he had sought and the justice he had fought for.

He saw in the camera's lens a reflection of himself, a man scarred by loss but also strengthened by it. He saw a man who had faced the darkness and emerged with a newfound purpose, a man who was determined to make a difference, to create a world where justice prevailed and truth was not a fleeting shadow but a guiding light.

He knew that the shadows of the past would always be a part of him, a constant reminder of the darkness that lurked within the human heart. But he also knew that within him, a spark of hope flickered, a belief that the world could be a better place, a world where truth and justice prevailed. And he was determined to keep that spark alive, to carry it forward, to shine its light on the darkness, one step at a time.

Chapter 11: The Unseen Connections

The weight of the past pressed down on John, a suffocating blanket of unanswered questions and lingering fears. He had found his sister's killer, brought him to justice, and finally laid her to rest. Yet, the truth, like a jagged shard, remained embedded in his heart. He couldn't shake the feeling that he had only scratched the surface, that the deeper mysteries of Sarah's disappearance remained elusive. His pursuit of justice had unearthed a tangled web of deceit, revealing a hidden world where darkness lurked beneath the veneer of normalcy.

He felt a growing compulsion to dig deeper, to confront the shadows of his past and find answers to the questions that had haunted him for so long. He had lived a life intertwined with his sister's, their childhood memories woven into the fabric of his being. Now, he realized, there were gaps in his recollection, events and relationships that he had forgotten or deliberately chosen to ignore.

He began to examine his childhood memories with renewed intensity, searching for connections to the events of Sarah's disappearance. He remembered their shared love of photography, Sarah's passion for capturing the fleeting moments of life through the lens of her camera. They had spent countless hours together, wandering through the woods behind their home, Sarah's camera clicking away, recording their adventures.

He recalled how they had discovered a hidden clearing, a secret sanctuary where they would escape from the pressures of their lives. He remembered the feeling of peace and serenity they had experienced there, the feeling of belonging to a world that was theirs alone.

But there were other memories, darker ones, that he had tried to bury deep within his subconscious. Memories of Sarah's growing isolation, her troubled relationship with their parents, and her increasing tendency to withdraw from the world. He had always attributed these changes to her teenage angst, but now he began to suspect there was something more.

He remembered a particularly vivid memory, a day when he had found Sarah sitting in their garden, her eyes filled with a sadness that he couldn't comprehend. She had been clutching a crumpled piece of paper, her fingers trembling as she tried to hide it from him. He had been too young to understand what she was going through, and he had never questioned her about it.

Now, as he revisited that memory, he realized that the paper she had been holding might have been a clue, a link to the events that would eventually lead to her disappearance. He had dismissed it as a teenage tantrum, but now he knew that he had been wrong.

He dug through old boxes and photo albums, searching for any evidence that might help him piece together Sarah's last days. He found a collection of Polaroid photos, captured by Sarah in the weeks leading up to her disappearance. They were mostly mundane snapshots, documenting her daily life: a cup of coffee, a book on her nightstand, a sunrise over the lake. But one photo stood out, a grainy image of a man standing in the shadows, his face obscured by darkness. He had been lurking in the background of Sarah's photos for weeks, his presence a constant reminder of a lurking danger.

John felt a shiver run down his spine as he stared at the photo. He recognized the man, a shadowy figure from his past, a man who had haunted their lives. He remembered him from their childhood, a friend of the family who had always been a little too close for comfort.

His name was David, and he had been a frequent visitor to their home, often spending hours with Sarah and John, engaging in conversations that were often too adult for their young minds. He had always been a charmer, a master of manipulation, a man who could win over even the most skeptical people with his charm and charisma.

John recalled how Sarah had grown increasingly uncomfortable with David's presence, how she had begun to avoid him at all costs. She had confided in John, expressing her fears and anxieties about his behavior. He had dismissed her concerns, telling her that David was just a harmless friend of the family.

But now, as he looked at the photo, he realized that he had been wrong. David's presence in Sarah's life was not harmless; it had been a calculated attempt to gain her trust and affection, a prelude to something far more sinister.

He remembered the day Sarah disappeared, a day that had forever changed their lives. He had been at school when he received a frantic phone call from their parents, his heart sinking as he listened to their tearful pleas. They had found a note left on Sarah's bed, a message written in her handwriting that said she was going for a walk in the woods behind their home. They had searched for her for hours, their pleas turning to despair as the sun began to set.

He had been too young to understand the gravity of the situation, but he had felt the weight of their sorrow, the fear that had gripped their hearts. The police had been called, and a full-scale search had been launched, but Sarah was nowhere to be found.

John had returned to the woods, his heart pounding with a mixture of fear and dread. He had searched every nook and cranny, calling out her name, hoping for a miracle. But all he found was a single photograph, lying on the forest floor, Sarah's camera lying beside it. It was a picture of a clearing in the woods, the same clearing they had discovered as children, a place where they had shared so many precious moments.

He had never questioned why the photograph was there, or why Sarah had taken it. But now, as he stared at it, he saw a faint figure in the background, a man standing near the edge of the clearing. The figure was too faint to make out, but John was certain it was David.

The realization hit him like a physical blow. David had

been lurking in the shadows, watching Sarah, waiting for his chance. The photo was not a random snapshot; it was a message, a warning, a reminder of the lurking danger that had been a constant presence in their lives.

The revelation sent a chill down his spine. He had been blind to the truth, blinded by his own assumptions and his fear of confronting the darkness within his family's past. He had allowed his sister's fear to be dismissed as teenage angst, her discomfort to be swept aside. He had been wrong, and his mistake had cost Sarah her life.

He vowed to do everything in his power to find the truth, to expose David's crimes and bring him to justice. He knew that it would be a long and dangerous journey, but he was determined to see it through to the end. He would confront the shadows of his past, face his demons, and seek justice for his sister. He would honor her memory by revealing the truth, even if it meant confronting the darkness within himself.

John stared at the worn photograph, the blurry image of a shadowy figure, a figure he now recognized as Peter. A jolt of realization ran through him, sending a shiver down his spine. Peter, the seemingly charming businessman, the man who had always been a presence in his life, had become the focus of his investigation. The revelation was a punch to the gut, a betrayal that felt personal, a violation of trust.

He recalled the countless times he had crossed paths with Peter, at social gatherings, charity events, and family dinners. They had always been cordial, even friendly, but now, every interaction felt tainted, every word spoken with a hidden agenda. The realization that Peter was not who he seemed, that beneath the facade of respectability lurked a calculating and dangerous mind, chilled him to the core.

John's thoughts raced back to the day Sarah disappeared. He remembered Peter's presence at the family gathering, his seemingly innocuous demeanor, his casual inquiries about Sarah's whereabouts. Suddenly, everything felt different, everything reinterpreted through the lens of suspicion. Was there something about Peter's behavior on that day that he had missed? A subtle shift in tone, a fleeting glance, a nervous tremor? The questions flooded his mind, each one a fresh stab of pain.

The investigation had revealed a history of animosity between his family and Peter's family. Their families had been intertwined for generations, their businesses entangled in a web of competition and rivalry. The feud had intensified when his father, a respected businessman, had outmaneuvered Peter's father in a crucial deal, a move that had left a bitter taste in the mouths of Peter's family. The animosity had been passed down through the generations, a simmering resentment that had festered for decades.

He unearthed old documents, dusty letters, and yellowed newspaper clippings, piecing together the fractured history of their families. He discovered that the rivalry had extended beyond business, spilling into personal lives, creating a cycle of mistrust and suspicion that had poisoned the relationship between the two families. John realized that Sarah's disappearance might not be an isolated incident but a culmination of years of simmering animosity.

He had been so focused on Sarah's personal relationships, her past, her secrets, that he had overlooked the larger picture, the legacy of bitterness that had shadowed their families for generations. His investigation had taken him down a rabbit hole, uncovering a dark underbelly of his own family history, a truth that he had chosen to ignore for so long.

John's mind raced back to the moment he had confronted Peter, the moment when the facade had crumbled, revealing the calculating and ruthless man beneath. Peter had denied any involvement in Sarah's disappearance, his voice laced with indignation and denial. But John had seen the flicker of fear in his eyes, the subtle twitch of his lips, the telltale signs of a man caught in a lie.

He knew that Peter had been involved in Sarah's disappearance, but he needed proof. He needed to tie Peter to the crime, to unravel the truth behind his actions. He began to revisit every detail, every piece of evidence, seeking a link, a connection that would cement Peter's involvement.

He discovered that Peter had been involved in a series of

shady business dealings, transactions that had been shrouded in secrecy and deception. He had used his influence and connections to manipulate the system, to enrich himself at the expense of others. John's suspicions grew with each new discovery, each piece of information that painted a darker picture of Peter's true nature.

The investigation had become a personal crusade, a quest for justice, not just for Sarah but for the generations who had been impacted by the rivalry between their families. John knew that uncovering the truth, exposing Peter's crimes, would be a long and arduous journey. He faced an adversary who was cunning, well-connected, and ruthless. But he was determined to see it through, to bring Peter to justice and to break the cycle of animosity that had plagued their families for so long.

He knew that the truth could be a dangerous weapon, a force that could shatter lives and expose hidden agendas. But he also knew that it was a force for good, a power that could liberate and heal. He was prepared to pay the price, to face the consequences, to stand against the shadows that had haunted their families for generations. His sister's disappearance had awakened a dormant sense of justice within him, a fire that burned with an intensity that surprised even him. He was ready to fight, to seek the truth, to bring justice to Sarah and to break the cycle of animosity that had poisoned their families for so long.

The weight of the secret pressed down on John like a physical burden. He'd spent years chasing shadows, uncovering buried truths, but this was different. This was a secret that ran deeper than any case he'd ever worked, a secret that resonated with the very core of his family history. It was a secret that, once unearthed, would irrevocably alter the course of his investigation and redefine his understanding of his family's past.

His journey began with a chance encounter, a faded photograph found clutched in the skeletal hand of his sister, Sarah. The photograph, a blurry snapshot of a fleeting moment, had become a talisman of his obsession. It was the only visual clue to Sarah's fate, a silent witness to a tragedy that had haunted his life for decades. The photo revealed a shadowy figure lurking behind Sarah, a figure John was certain he recognized, but couldn't quite place.

He'd spent countless hours staring at the image, meticulously analyzing every detail, searching for a piece of the puzzle that would unlock the mystery of Sarah's disappearance. And yet, despite his relentless pursuit, the truth remained elusive, concealed behind a veil of fragmented memories and unspoken truths. The photo had ignited a fire within him, a desperate yearning for answers. But it also ignited a fear, a gnawing dread that the truth might be too painful to bear.

As John delved deeper into his family's history, he discovered a tapestry of secrets woven into the fabric of their lives. They weren't just secrets of infidelity or hidden wealth, they were secrets that had the power to shatter lives and leave scars that time could not heal. His family's history was a labyrinth of deceit and manipulation, a labyrinth that John now found himself lost within.

His investigation had taken him down a winding path, leading him to suspects who had been carefully cultivated, their motives hidden behind masks of innocence. The trail of deception had led him to the fringes of society, to individuals whose lives were shrouded in shadows, their secrets buried deep beneath layers of lies.

He'd uncovered a web of connections, a intricate dance of guilt and innocence, where the lines between truth and fabrication blurred with each passing day. It was a dance that he was determined to unravel, even if it meant confronting the demons of his own past. He had to find answers, not just for his own sanity, but for Sarah's memory, for the family he loved, and for the justice he sought to restore.

The secret he uncovered was a truth so profound that it left him reeling. It was a truth that had been concealed for generations, buried beneath the weight of unspoken words and hidden intentions. It was a truth that explained the motives behind the actions of those involved, a truth that illuminated the darker corners of his family's history.

The secret was a revelation that cast a long shadow over

his life, a revelation that forced him to confront the darkest aspects of his family's past. It was a revelation that would forever change his understanding of his family, his world, and himself.

The truth he had been desperately seeking, the truth he had been willing to sacrifice everything for, was a truth that shattered the world he had known. It was a truth that revealed the depths of human depravity and the lengths to which people would go to protect their secrets.

The weight of the revelation threatened to crush him, but he knew he had to keep going. He had to face the truth, however painful it might be, for the sake of his sister, for the sake of his family, and for the sake of justice.

The secret, once revealed, would set in motion a chain of events that would forever alter the course of his life. He knew it would be a dangerous journey, a journey fraught with danger and uncertainty. But he was determined to see it through to the end. He would not rest until the truth was revealed, until the shadows were banished from his family's past, and until justice was served.

John's quest for answers led him down a winding path, each step revealing a new layer of truth. The initial investigation focused on the immediate circle of suspects, those closest to Sarah. However, his instincts told him that the truth lay deeper, hidden beneath layers of deceit. His relentless pursuit of justice, fueled by a desire to honor Sarah's memory, led him to a hidden archive, a dusty repository of old documents and records, tucked away in a forgotten corner of the city library.

The archive was a sanctuary for forgotten stories, a graveyard of secrets whispered through time. It housed the forgotten whispers of the city, the voices of those who had gone unheard, their stories locked away in yellowed pages and faded ink. John spent days immersed in the archive, sifting through dusty volumes, his fingers tracing the faded ink of long-lost narratives. He felt a strange connection to these forgotten souls, their stories mirroring his own quest for truth.

As he delved deeper, he unearthed evidence that pointed to a hidden society, a secret organization operating in the shadows, their influence reaching into every corner of the city. Their existence was shrouded in secrecy, their motives veiled in obscurity. The group, referred to only as "The Order" in the archive, had been manipulating events for decades, their actions leaving a trail of hidden agendas and broken lives in their wake.

The Order was comprised of influential individuals from various walks of life, connected by a shared desire for power and control. They had infiltrated the city's institutions, wielding their influence to manipulate markets, control elections, and orchestrate events to their advantage. Their activities were shrouded in secrecy, their operations conducted through a network of coded messages and secret meetings.

Their modus operandi was insidious, using their wealth and influence to sway public opinion, silence dissent, and suppress any threat to their control. Their grip on the city was like a silent vise, slowly squeezing the life out of those who dared to oppose them.

John's discovery of The Order sent shockwaves through his investigation. His quest for justice had taken a drastic turn, evolving into a fight against a formidable force. He felt a surge of fear mixed with a fierce determination to expose The Order's crimes. His personal quest for justice for Sarah had transformed into a fight for the very soul of the city.

As he delved deeper into The Order's activities, he discovered Sarah's involvement with the group. She had stumbled upon their illegal activities, witnessing their manipulations firsthand. Driven by a sense of justice and a desire to expose their crimes, she had begun investigating them on her own.

John's heart sank as he realized the depth of Sarah's bravery. He had always known his sister as a kind and compassionate soul, but her actions revealed a hidden strength, a fierce determination to fight for what she believed in. He understood now that Sarah's disappearance was no mere coincidence. She had been a threat to The Order, her investigation a dangerous game of cat and mouse that had ended tragically.

The Order had silenced her, their motive to protect their power and maintain control. Her demise was a chilling reminder of the lengths to which they would go to protect their secrets. John's grief was compounded by the realization that Sarah's death was not an isolated incident. The Order had a long history of silencing those who crossed their path, their victims forgotten, their stories lost to time.

John felt a weight settling on his shoulders, a responsibility to honor Sarah's memory by exposing The Order's crimes and bringing them to justice. He realized that his investigation was no longer just about finding Sarah's killer; it was about protecting the innocent and holding the powerful accountable.

As he pieced together the fragments of The Order's past, a chilling truth emerged. The group had been manipulating events for generations, their tentacles reaching back into the city's history, influencing the course of its development and shaping the lives of its inhabitants. Their involvement in Sarah's disappearance was just the tip of the iceberg, their crimes far more extensive than John could have imagined.

His discovery of The Order had irrevocably changed the direction of his investigation. It had transformed a personal quest for justice into a fight against a formidable enemy, a fight that would challenge everything he knew and test the very limits of his resilience. But John was determined to fight for truth, for justice, and for his sister's memory, no matter the cost.

John's heart pounded against his ribs, a frantic drumbeat

echoing the urgency of the situation. He stared at the worn, leather-bound journal, its pages filled with Sarah's elegant script. The words danced before his eyes, a swirling kaleidoscope of memories and revelations. He had spent weeks meticulously piecing together the fragments of his sister's life, chasing shadows in the darkness, and now, here in the heart of this hidden archive, he felt the weight of truth crushing him.

He traced his finger across the faded ink, his mind grappling with the gravity of Sarah's words. It was a diary, a sanctuary for her innermost thoughts and fears, a secret world she had kept hidden from him and the rest of their family. It was a world of shadows, a world of whispers and secret societies.

The pages detailed Sarah's investigation, her growing unease as she delved deeper into the heart of a clandestine organization, a web of power and corruption that had seeped into every fiber of society. He read with bated breath, his stomach churning with a mix of horror and despair. Sarah had stumbled upon a conspiracy so insidious, so pervasive, that it had been operating in the shadows for decades, pulling the strings of power, manipulating events, and silencing anyone who dared to expose their secrets.

She had unearthed a network of individuals who wielded influence, who had infiltrated the highest echelons of power, who controlled the flow of information, and who held a grip on the very fabric of society. Their influence stretched across industries, across governments, and across the very borders of the nation. They operated with an air of impunity, their power a silent, menacing force that controlled the levers of society from the shadows.

John's mind raced as he read, trying to make sense of the tangled web of names, dates, and locations. Sarah had meticulously documented her findings, leaving a trail of breadcrumbs for him to follow. Each page was a chilling testament to her courage, her dedication to exposing the truth, and her unwavering belief in justice. She had put her life on the line to bring these criminals to light.

He paused, his eyes falling on a passage that sent a shiver down his spine. Sarah had been closing in on their leader, a shadowy figure known only as "The Weaver," who pulled the strings of this vast network of corruption. Sarah had been documenting their meetings, their plans, and their motivations, her life hanging in the balance as she risked everything to expose their secrets.

His gaze lingered on the final entry, dated the night of Sarah's disappearance. She had written about a confrontation, a meeting with The Weaver, a desperate plea for help. The last words were barely decipherable, a frantic scribble that spoke of danger, of a desperate escape, and a chilling sense of foreboding.

John felt a wave of grief wash over him, a wave of sorrow for his sister and the tragic fate that had befallen her. She had been so close, so close to exposing the truth, only to be silenced by the very forces she was trying to bring down.

He closed the journal, the weight of its contents settling in his chest. He knew, with a certainty that chilled him to the bone, that the secret society had been responsible for Sarah's disappearance. They had seen her as a threat, an obstacle to their plans, and they had taken her out, silencing her forever.

The realization was a blow, a crushing weight that threatened to drown him in despair. But as the initial shock subsided, a spark of defiance ignited within him. He would not let Sarah's sacrifice be in vain. He would honor her memory, he would carry her torch, and he would bring these criminals to justice.

He stood, his resolve hardening as he looked at the weathered pages of the journal. It was a chilling testament to his sister's bravery, her dedication, and her unwavering pursuit of truth. He would follow her lead, he would uncover their secrets, and he would bring them to light.

The discovery of the secret society had thrown him into a new world, a world of shadows and secrets, a world of conspiracies and deceit. It was a world far beyond what he had ever imagined, a world where the lines between right and wrong blurred, where justice was often elusive, and where the truth was buried beneath layers of lies.

But he was determined to bring the truth to light, to expose the darkness that had consumed his sister and to hold those responsible for her death accountable. He would fight for justice, he would fight for Sarah, and he would fight for the soul of his nation.

John left the archive, a weight of responsibility settling on his shoulders. He had a new mission, a mission to expose the secret society and bring them to justice. He would carry his sister's torch, he would uncover the truth, and he would fight for the future of his nation.

His journey had taken him down a dark and twisted path, but he was determined to find his way out, to shine a light on the darkness, and to bring justice to those who had been wronged. He would not rest until he had brought Sarah's killers to justice, until he had exposed the truth, and until he had restored faith in the power of justice.

Chapter 12: The Pursuit of Truth

John's heart pounded in his chest, a rhythm mirroring the escalating urgency that had taken hold of him. The weight of his discovery, the existence of a clandestine society operating in the shadows, pressed down on him with crushing force. He had spent years chasing the ghost of his sister's disappearance, driven by a love that refused to be silenced. Now, the truth had revealed itself, but it was a truth far more sinister, more pervasive, than he could have ever imagined.

These were not just random acts of violence or isolated acts of cruelty. This was a carefully orchestrated web of deception, a tapestry woven from threads of power, greed, and manipulation. They had been manipulating events, influencing the lives of countless individuals, pulling strings from the shadows, all while cloaked in an aura of respectability.

The realization hit him like a physical blow. They had been operating for years, maybe even decades, their influence reaching far and wide. Their network extended into every corner of society, like a virus spreading its insidious tendrils. He could see it now, the whispers of their influence in the political circles, the hushed conversations in the boardrooms of major corporations, the subtle manipulations of public opinion.

John felt a surge of anger course through his veins, a righteous fury that ignited a fire within him. They had taken his sister, they had stolen countless lives, and he was not going to let them get away with it. He was no longer just a detective seeking closure for a personal tragedy; he was a soldier in a battle against darkness. He would expose them, he would bring them down, even if it cost him everything.

The dangers involved were immense, but the thought of backing down was unthinkable. They were powerful, well-connected, and ruthless, but John was not afraid. He had faced down countless adversaries in his career, and he knew how to fight. This was not about personal gain, this was about justice, about righting a wrong that had haunted him for far too long.

He had spent years chasing shadows, searching for a glimmer of light in the darkness. Now, the darkness had revealed itself, and he was determined to fight back. He would not be deterred, he would not be silenced. He would become the voice of the voiceless, the champion of the oppressed, the harbinger of truth.

The pursuit of justice was a perilous path, but John was not one to shy away from a challenge. He had spent his life battling for what was right, and he was not about to abandon his principles now. The memory of his sister, her vibrant smile and her infectious laughter, fueled his resolve. He owed it to her, to all the victims of their machinations, to bring them down.

John knew that his quest was far from over. The fight would be long and arduous, filled with obstacles and setbacks. But he would not falter, he would not give in. The secret society had underestimated him, they had underestimated the power of a man driven by love, justice, and an unwavering belief in the truth.

He would not rest until their crimes were exposed, their influence shattered, and their power broken. This was his mission, his crusade, and he would not stop until justice was served. The shadow of the past had haunted him for years, but now he was ready to confront it, to banish it from the world, and to finally find peace.

John's phone buzzed on the desk, snapping him back to reality. It was a message from Sarah's old friend, Emily, who had been a key witness in the investigation. She had been missing for weeks, and John had a bad feeling about it.

"I have something you need to see," the message read, followed by a link to an online file.

John's heart sank. He had a feeling that Emily had stumbled upon something dangerous, something that had put her in the crosshairs of the secret society. He had to find her, he had to protect her. But first, he had to see what she had found.

He clicked the link, his mind racing. The file was a video, a shaky recording of what appeared to be a secret meeting. The faces of the individuals in the video were obscured, but their voices were clear.

The words were chilling: "We need to eliminate her, she knows too much."

John's blood ran cold. This was it, the proof he needed. The secret society was willing to kill to protect their secrets. But who was "her?"

John had to find Emily. He had to find her fast.

He spent the next few hours frantically scouring the city, searching for any trace of her. He checked her apartment, her office, even her favorite haunts. There was nothing. The only clue he had was a message from her, sent shortly before she disappeared, that simply read: "They're watching."

The words sent a shiver down his spine. He was not alone in this fight. He had to protect himself, but he also had to find Emily. They needed each other.

John's pursuit of truth had taken a dangerous turn. The secret society was not just a group of criminals, they were a powerful force, a shadow government operating in plain sight. They were willing to do whatever it took to maintain their power, and they were not afraid to silence those who threatened to expose them.

John knew he was facing an uphill battle, but he was not going to back down. He was going to find Emily, he was going to expose their crimes, and he was going to bring them down. The pursuit of truth was a dangerous path, but it was a path that he was willing to walk, even if it meant sacrificing everything.

John's pursuit of the truth led him down a treacherous rabbit hole, a journey that revealed the insidious reach of the secret society. He had stumbled upon a hidden network of power, a shadowy cabal that had infiltrated the very foundations of society. Their influence was pervasive, reaching into government agencies, corporate boardrooms, and even law enforcement, their tentacles wrapped tightly around the levers of power.

The more John unearthed, the more unsettling the truth became. The society's influence was subtle, a whisper in the corridors of power, a nudge here, a veiled threat there. They operated in the shadows, their actions masked by layers of deceit and manipulation. John discovered that they had infiltrated government agencies, planting their operatives in key positions, shaping policies and agendas to suit their nefarious agenda. Their presence extended to the corporate world, where they had leveraged their influence to gain control of strategic industries, manipulating markets and exploiting resources for their own gain. The society had even infiltrated law enforcement, corrupting officers and turning them into unwitting pawns in their game of control.

John was stunned by the depth of their influence. The society's reach was far greater than he had ever imagined, and their grip on power was stronger than he had dared to believe. They had woven a web of deceit, using money, blackmail, and violence to silence their opponents and ensure their continued dominance. Their network of influence was vast, a tangled tapestry of connections that extended to every corner of society.

John's investigation led him to a series of high-profile figures, individuals who held positions of power and influence. He discovered that they were not merely pawns in the society's game but active players, complicit in its schemes. They had embraced the society's dark ideology, believing that they were part of a higher purpose, a force that would usher in a new era of control and order. John was horrified by their arrogance and their willingness to sacrifice the well-being of others for their own ambition.

John's pursuit of truth had taken a personal toll. The weight of the secret society's crimes, the corruption he had witnessed, and the danger he faced had taken their toll. He was haunted by the knowledge of the society's influence, knowing that they had touched every aspect of his life, manipulating events and influencing decisions. He was no longer sure who to trust, who was playing by the rules, and who was part of the game.

John's investigation had also shaken his faith in the institutions he had once believed in. He realized that the very foundations of society were built on lies and corruption. He had seen how easily power could be manipulated, how easily people could be controlled, and how readily individuals would turn a blind eye to injustice for the sake of personal gain.

He had to keep pushing forward, however. The truth demanded it. He was driven by a sense of duty, a responsibility to expose the secret society's crimes and bring them to justice. He knew that his investigation had put him on a collision course with a powerful and dangerous enemy. He was aware of the risks, the potential consequences of exposing the truth, but he was not deterred. He had seen the victims, the innocent people whose lives had been destroyed by the society's actions. He owed it to them, to his sister, and to himself to fight back.

John's relentless pursuit of the truth had not gone unnoticed. The secret society had become aware of his investigation and had made it clear that he would face dire consequences if he did not back down. They had sent their agents after him, threatening his life and the lives of his loved ones. John was forced to go into hiding, constantly looking over his shoulder, knowing that the society's reach was vast and their methods ruthless.

Despite the risks, John refused to back down. He had seen too much, known too much, to simply turn a blind eye. He had a responsibility to expose the truth, to warn the world of the society's insidious influence. He knew that he was in a fight for his life, but he was not afraid. He had found a strength within himself, a resilience that he had never known existed. He was fueled by the memory of his sister, the love for his family, and a burning desire for justice. He was ready to fight.

John's investigation had taken him down a rabbit hole of

deceit and corruption. It was as if the entire city was built upon a foundation of lies, each brick carefully placed to obscure the truth. He had started with the disappearance of his sister, Sarah, but the deeper he dug, the more he realized that her case was only a single thread in a vast and intricate tapestry of corruption.

He started to see the connections, the whispers in the shadows, the subtle ways in which power was wielded and manipulated. He found evidence of a system of checks and balances, a web of relationships designed to maintain a carefully constructed facade of order. The people he had known, the faces he had seen every day, were now suspect, their true motives hidden behind layers of masks and pretenses.

He had been following the trail of the secret society, the group of individuals who had been manipulating events behind the scenes. He had discovered that they were deeply embedded in the fabric of the city, their tentacles reaching into every corner, controlling the levers of power from the shadows.

He uncovered evidence of their influence, of their cunning machinations, and their ability to operate with impunity. They had built a system of protection, a web of silence that shielded them from scrutiny and accountability. Their power rested not only on their wealth and influence but also on their ability to intimidate and manipulate those who dared to cross them.

He began to understand the source of their power. They used fear, bribery, and blackmail to keep their influence. They exploited people's vulnerabilities, turning them into pawns in their game of power. They had created a system of dependence, a web of entanglements that made it difficult for anyone to escape their control.

John realized that this secret society was a threat not only to his sister, but to the entire city. They were a cancer, spreading their corruption and undermining the very foundations of society. He felt a surge of anger, a determination to expose their crimes and bring them to justice.

He knew the risks involved. This wasn't just a case of solving a crime; it was a battle against a powerful enemy, an enemy who had built a system of protection around itself, who had the resources and the influence to make him disappear.

John had discovered the web of corruption, but it had also trapped him. He was now caught in a web of his own, struggling to navigate a treacherous path where every step could be his last. The pursuit of truth had become a deadly game, a fight for survival. He was no longer just a detective; he was a warrior, fighting against the darkness that had consumed his city.

He had to fight, not just for his sister, but for the people of his city, for the future of a world where truth and justice could prevail. It was a daunting task, a battle against seemingly insurmountable odds. But he was not one to back down from a challenge. He had a fire in his soul, a burning desire to bring those responsible to justice, to expose the truth, no matter the cost.

The pursuit of truth was a dangerous game, but it was a game he was willing to play. He had seen too much, he had felt too much, he had been driven by a thirst for justice that could not be quenched. He would not rest until he had brought down the secret society, until he had exposed their crimes, and until he had brought peace to a city that had been consumed by darkness.

John was no longer just a detective, he was a crusader, a champion of truth and justice, fighting for the soul of his city. He had crossed a line, a point of no return. He had seen the darkness, and he had chosen to fight it. His quest for truth had become a quest for survival, a battle for the very heart of his city. He was no longer alone; he had allies, individuals who had also been touched by the secret society's darkness, who had also been forced to fight back. They were a ragtag group, united by a common enemy, a common goal.

John knew that their fight would be long and difficult, but he was determined to see it through to the end. He was a warrior for truth, and he would not surrender. He had to keep moving forward, to keep fighting, to keep exposing the truth, no matter the cost. He had to win, not just for himself, but for all those who had been victims of the secret society's corruption, for the future of a city that desperately needed to be cleansed of the darkness that had taken root within its soul.

John stood on the edge of a precipice, the wind whipping at his face, carrying the scent of salt and the distant roar of the ocean. His gaze was fixed on the horizon, the vast expanse mirroring the turmoil within him. For months, he'd been chasing shadows, piecing together a fragmented reality, the truth of his sister's disappearance slowly revealing itself, layer by layer, like peeling back the skin of an onion. Each revelation brought a new wave of pain, a fresh wound to an already scarred heart.

The investigation had taken him to the darkest corners of his city, into the shadowy recesses of human depravity, exposing a world where power and greed ruled, where morality was a mere suggestion, easily discarded in the pursuit of self-interest. He'd unmasked the perpetrator, a man who hid behind a facade of normalcy, a wolf in sheep's clothing, his true nature concealed until the weight of the truth finally crushed the carefully crafted illusion.

But the truth, as it often does, had opened a Pandora's box, revealing a web of corruption that extended far beyond the initial case. He had stumbled upon a secret society, an insidious network of powerful individuals who operated in the shadows, pulling the strings of society from behind the scenes. Their influence was like a malignant tumor, spreading its tendrils into every facet of life, distorting reality and bending the rules to their will.

John had glimpsed the dark underbelly of the city, the

hidden machinations of those who sought to control, to manipulate, to exploit. He knew their existence, their purpose, their methods. He knew the dangers involved in exposing them, the price he might pay for revealing their secrets. But his sister's memory burned bright, a beacon illuminating his path, guiding him towards the righteous path, no matter the cost.

A sense of righteous anger coursed through him, fueled by the injustice he'd witnessed, the lives destroyed, the truth buried under layers of deceit. He'd dedicated his life to upholding the law, to seeking justice for those who had been wronged, to protecting the innocent. And now, he faced a choice: To remain silent, to turn a blind eye to the insidious corruption, or to stand up, to fight, to risk everything in pursuit of a truth that threatened to consume him.

The choice was agonizing, a moral dilemma that gnawed at his conscience, a battle between fear and duty. He knew the risks, the potential consequences. The secret society held immense power, their reach extended into every corner of the city, their influence wielded with a chilling efficiency that chilled his bones.

He had seen them operate, their methods subtle yet devastating, their motives shrouded in secrecy. He knew they wouldn't hesitate to eliminate anyone who threatened their power, to silence those who dared to speak the truth. The threat was real, tangible, a palpable shadow looming over him, a constant reminder of the dangers he faced.

He considered his options, weighing the risks against the potential rewards. He could retreat, disappear, become another silent victim, another pawn in their game. Or he could stand up, fight back, become a voice for the voiceless, a champion of justice. He knew the odds were stacked against him, that the fight would be a perilous journey, but he refused to succumb to fear.

His sister's face flashed in his mind, her eyes filled with a mixture of mischief and wisdom. He remembered her laugh, her warm embrace, the love she'd shared with him. He remembered her strength, her courage, her unwavering belief in truth and justice. He knew she wouldn't want him to back down, to surrender to fear. She'd demand he fight, to use his skills, his knowledge, his determination to expose the darkness, to bring justice to light.

He took a deep breath, the salty air filling his lungs, a reminder of the vastness of the world, the countless lives intertwined, the delicate balance that could be shattered in an instant. He understood the gravity of the decision he faced, the weight of the responsibility he carried. He knew the risks, the potential consequences, but he also knew the importance of his mission, the lives that could be saved, the truth that needed to be revealed.

He turned his back on the vast expanse of the ocean, the setting sun painting the sky in hues of orange and purple. He felt a renewed sense of purpose, a determination that burned bright within him. He would face the shadows, confront the darkness, and bring justice to light, no matter the cost. He would stand up, fight back, and become a voice for those who had been silenced, a champion of truth. He would honor his sister's memory, her courage, her unwavering belief in justice. He would fight, he would win, and he would expose the truth.

John felt the weight of his resolve settle deep within him, like a heavy stone grounding him in the face of an unforgiving storm. He was no longer just a detective seeking justice for his sister; he was a warrior in a war against a formidable enemy, a secret society that had burrowed its way into the very fabric of society. The truth he sought was no longer a personal quest for closure; it was a beacon of hope for a world shrouded in darkness.

The realization of the society's insidious influence was a chilling revelation. He had seen glimpses of its tendrils reaching into every corner of life, from the halls of government to the boardrooms of corporations. They moved in the shadows, pulling strings and orchestrating events, their motives shrouded in a veil of secrecy. They were a hydra, with countless heads, each one representing a different facet of their corrupt system.

He knew they were formidable, a force with resources far beyond his reach, but he refused to be cowed. His sister's memory was a constant reminder of the stakes involved. Sarah had been silenced, a victim of their power and greed, but her legacy would not be forgotten. Her voice would be heard, even if it meant risking everything.

The fear that had once gnawed at him, a constant reminder of his vulnerability, now felt like a distant echo. He was no longer simply seeking justice for his sister; he was fighting for a world where truth could prevail, where the forces of darkness could be vanquished. The weight of this responsibility, this burden of hope, filled him with a newfound determination.

He started by building his own network, reaching out to others who had been touched by the society's corrupt hand. He discovered a small but dedicated group of individuals, each with their own stories of betrayal and loss, who were determined to fight back. They were the silent witnesses, the voices that had been silenced, the souls who had been robbed of their freedom.

He began to gather information, piecing together the fragments of a puzzle that revealed a tapestry of corruption. He uncovered evidence of their illegal activities, their manipulation of markets, their infiltration of government agencies, and their brutal silencing of anyone who dared to oppose them. Their reach was vast, their power immense, but John knew that their strength lay in their secrecy.

The thought of exposing them, of bringing their darkness into the light, filled him with both trepidation and exhilaration. He knew the risks involved, the potential consequences. He could lose his job, his reputation, his life. But the thought of turning away, of letting them continue their reign of terror, was unbearable. He had seen the darkness, the suffering they inflicted, and he couldn't live with himself if he didn't fight back.

He knew he was facing an impossible task, a David versus Goliath battle, but he was not alone. He had allies, a small but determined group who believed in the power of truth. He had his own inner strength, fueled by his sister's memory, his own sense of justice, and a deep-seated belief that good would ultimately prevail.

He knew the journey ahead would be fraught with danger, but he was ready to face it. The weight of responsibility settled upon him, a reminder of the lives at stake, the fight for a brighter future. He would expose the society's secrets, he would bring their corrupt system crashing down, and he would ensure that Sarah's voice, along with the voices of all those they had silenced, would finally be heard. He was driven by a burning desire for justice, a relentless pursuit of truth, and a belief in the power of hope to light the way even in the darkest of times.

Chapter 13: The Price of Truth

The chill of the city's night air clung to John's skin as he raced through the deserted streets, the weight of his investigation pressing down on him like a physical burden. Every shadow seemed to hold a lurking danger, every sound a potential threat. The secret society's agents, driven by a ruthless hunger for silence, were on his trail, and John knew that every moment was precious. He had stumbled upon a truth that was too dangerous to be ignored, a truth that threatened to unravel the very fabric of society. He had dared to look into the abyss, and now the abyss stared back, its cold, malevolent gaze seeking to extinguish the light of his resolve.

He had been running for days, his once-familiar city now a maze of twisting alleys and shadowy corners, each one a potential ambush point. The constant fear, the relentless paranoia, gnawed at his sanity, chipping away at the man he used to be. He had sought answers, driven by the desperate need to find justice for his sister, Sarah. He had believed in the sanctity of truth, the power of justice to right the wrongs of the world. But the deeper he had delved into the case, the more he had realized the extent of the corruption that festered beneath the surface of society. The secret society, a clandestine network of power and influence, had woven its tentacles into every corner of the city, silencing dissent and controlling the flow of information.

John knew that they had been watching him, studying his

every move, waiting for the opportune moment to strike. He had been naive to believe that he could expose their secrets and walk away unscathed. They were not a group of ordinary criminals; they were masters of the shadows, experts in manipulation and deceit. They had been operating for decades, their tentacles extending into every aspect of society, their power vast and their reach seemingly infinite.

The pressure was immense. The weight of his sister's case, the fear of his own mortality, and the knowledge that his actions were threatening a power structure that had remained unchallenged for far too long weighed heavily on his mind. But John was not one to back down from a fight. He knew that the truth was out there, waiting to be revealed. He had a duty to Sarah, to the victims of the secret society, and to himself to see this through.

He knew the risks, but he was willing to take them. He had stared into the face of darkness, and he refused to blink. The secret society was a powerful adversary, but John was not without his own strengths. He had a sharp mind, a keen eye for detail, and an unwavering determination to uncover the truth. He had spent his life chasing shadows, and now he was determined to bring those shadows to light. He had a weapon: his relentless pursuit of justice.

He knew that he had become a target, but that only made him more determined. He had to expose the secrets of the secret society, to bring their crimes to light, and to hold them accountable for their actions. He had seen the darkness, and he knew that only by confronting it could he hope to overcome it. He was no longer just a detective; he was a warrior, fighting for a world where truth and justice prevailed.

John pushed himself harder, his body screaming in protest, but he refused to yield. He knew that the agents were closing in, their pursuit becoming more relentless with each passing hour. He couldn't afford to stop, couldn't allow himself to be caught. The fate of his sister, the victims of the secret society, and the future of the city rested on his shoulders. He had to find a way to expose them, to break their hold on the city, to free it from the grip of their shadows.

He found himself in a decaying warehouse district, a labyrinth of rusted metal and broken concrete. He had been tipped off that this was a gathering place for the society's agents, a hub where they exchanged information and planned their next moves. He knew that he was walking into a trap, but he had to take the risk. He needed information, and he needed to gather evidence that could bring the society down.

He slipped into the warehouse, his movements silent and precise. The air was thick with the scent of decay and danger, the flickering light of a single bare bulb barely illuminating the shadows that danced in the corners of the vast space. He could hear the murmur of voices, the clinking of glasses, the low thrum of an unseen presence. He knew that he had to be careful, that one wrong move could spell his doom.

He edged his way through the darkness, his senses heightened, listening for any sign of danger. He had to find the source of the society's power, the heart of their network, the place where they made their decisions and executed their plans. He knew that the agents were everywhere, their eyes watching, their ears listening, waiting for any sign of a threat.

Suddenly, he heard a sharp intake of breath, the sound of a weapon being drawn. He froze, his body tensed, ready to react. A figure stepped out of the shadows, silhouetted against the faint light of the single bulb. The figure was tall and imposing, its face obscured by the darkness.

"John Snider," the figure spoke, its voice low and menacing, "We've been expecting you."

John felt a chill run down his spine. He knew that he had been caught, that his time was running out. The agents had been waiting for him, anticipating his arrival, ready to end his investigation once and for all.

"Who are you?" John asked, his voice calm despite the tremor that ran through his body. He had to keep his cool, had to buy himself time.

"That's not important," the figure replied, "What's important is that you stop what you're doing. You're digging into something you shouldn't be involved in. You're a threat to our organization, and we will not hesitate to eliminate that threat."

John knew that the agent was telling the truth. He had stumbled upon something far bigger than he had ever imagined, a web of corruption and deceit that threatened the very foundations of the city. But he was not ready to give up, not yet. He had come too far, risked too much, to be silenced now.

"I'm not going to stop," John replied, his voice firm, "I'm going to expose you. I'm going to bring you down."

The agent laughed, a cold, chilling sound that echoed through the warehouse. "You're a fool, Snider," he said, "You're playing a game you can't win. You think you can fight us? We're everywhere. We control everything. You're nothing but a pawn in our game, and you will be sacrificed when your usefulness is over."

John felt a surge of anger rise within him. He was no pawn. He was a man, a detective, and he had a responsibility to expose the truth, to bring justice to the victims of the secret society.

"You may be right," John replied, his voice laced with a dangerous edge, "But you've underestimated me. I'm not going down without a fight."

The agent drew his weapon, its metallic glint reflecting in the dim light. "Then you've chosen your fate, Snider."

John's heart pounded in his chest, his mind racing. He had no choice but to fight. The agent rushed at him, the glint of his weapon a deadly beacon in the darkness.

John dodged the attack, diving out of the way as the agent's bullet whizzed past his ear. He scrambled to his feet, adrenaline coursing through his veins, his mind focused on survival. He had to find a way out, had to escape the clutches of the secret society, had to stay alive long enough to bring their crimes to light.

He knew he had to get out of there, had to get away from the agent. He needed to find a way to alert the authorities, to expose the secret society, to bring them to justice. He had to survive long enough to tell his story, to make the world aware of the darkness that lurked beneath the surface of their city. He knew that he was running out of time, that the agents were closing in, that he had to act fast. He was on a mission, a dangerous, desperate mission, to bring the truth to light. And he was determined to see it through, no matter the cost.

John felt a chill run down his spine as he stared at the blurry photo, the image of Sarah, his sister, frozen in time, a ghostly reminder of her tragic fate. It was a stark reminder of the unseen enemy that had haunted his life for decades.

He was no longer just chasing the shadows of Sarah's disappearance; he was now on the trail of a clandestine organization, a hidden network of individuals who operated in the dark recesses of society. They were the architects of Sarah's demise, the puppet masters behind the tragedies that had befallen others like him.

John had stumbled upon a hidden truth, a secret that

had been buried deep within the fabric of society. The secret society had been manipulating events for years, influencing lives, and pulling strings from the shadows. Their agenda was shrouded in secrecy, their motives a twisted web of greed, power, and control.

His investigation had unearthed a horrifying truth: the secret society had been targeting individuals who posed a threat to their operations, those who dared to speak out against their corruption, those who held the key to their downfall. John was one of them. Sarah, his sister, had been another.

As John delved deeper, he discovered that he wasn't alone in his struggle. There were others who had been touched by the society's wicked hand, others who had witnessed their insidious actions and had been forced to flee for their lives. They were scattered like shards of a shattered mirror, hidden in the shadows, fearing for their safety.

John learned that the society had a systematic way of silencing their enemies. They would manipulate events, orchestrate accidents, or simply disappear their targets, leaving no trace, no evidence, no whispers of their existence. They were the masters of deceit, the purveyors of fear, and their tentacles stretched far and wide, reaching into every corner of society.

A wave of dread washed over John as he realized the true scope of the threat he faced. The secret society was a hydra, with many heads, each one more dangerous than the last. He was facing an enemy that was more powerful than any he had ever encountered, an enemy that played by its own rules, an enemy that operated in the shadows.

John's phone rang, breaking the silence that had descended upon his small apartment. He glanced at the caller ID: an unknown number. A surge of apprehension coursed through him. Could it be another victim? Was the secret society finally catching up to him?

He hesitated for a moment before answering.

"Hello?" he answered cautiously.

"John Snider?" a raspy voice asked.

John felt a cold knot form in his stomach.

"Yes, it's John."

"I'm a friend of Sarah's," the voice said, its tone laced with a hint of sadness. "I know about the society. I've been watching. I have information that can help you."

John felt a glimmer of hope. This could be a crucial lead, a lifeline in the darkness.

"Who is this? Where are you?" he asked urgently.

"Meet me at the old lighthouse. Tonight. Midnight. Come alone."

The voice hung up before John could ask another question. The lighthouse stood at the edge of town, a solitary sentinel overlooking the vast expanse of the ocean. It was a place of mystery and intrigue, a place where secrets were whispered on the wind.

John knew the risks involved. The secret society had been watching his every move, tracking his every step. But he couldn't ignore this opportunity. The thought of Sarah, of her suffering, of the lives that had been shattered by this organization, spurred him forward. He had to take this chance.

As the clock ticked past eleven, John found himself driving towards the lighthouse, his heart pounding in his chest. The wind howled, the waves crashed against the shore, and the only light came from the moon, a silver sliver hanging in the sky.

John parked his car at the base of the lighthouse, his eyes scanning the darkness. He could feel the weight of the world on his shoulders. He was alone, facing an unseen enemy. He was walking into the lion's den, but he was determined to uncover the truth, no matter the cost.

He climbed the winding stairs of the lighthouse, his footsteps echoing through the stone structure. The air was thick with the scent of salt and dampness. He reached the top, the viewing platform overlooking the ocean.

The wind whipped around him, carrying the scent of

brine and the sound of crashing waves. He scanned the horizon, searching for a sign of his mysterious contact.

Suddenly, a figure emerged from the shadows, shrouded in darkness.

"John?" the figure said, their voice barely a whisper.

John squinted, trying to make out the person in the darkness.

"Yes," he replied.

The figure took a step closer, revealing a face that was hidden behind a tattered scarf. Their eyes met John's, and a chill ran down his spine.

"I know you're looking for the truth, John," the figure said, their voice a low growl. "I know you're trying to expose the society. I can help you."

John felt a surge of hope, a flicker of light in the darkness. But he couldn't shake the feeling that something was amiss. There was something about this encounter, something that didn't feel right.

"What do you know?" he asked cautiously.

The figure smiled, a chilling, sinister smile that illuminated the darkness.

"More than you can imagine, John," they whispered.

"More than you can handle."

John's heart hammered against his ribs as he stood before the makeshift gathering. The victims of the clandestine society, each bearing their own scars of manipulation and abuse, their eyes reflecting a shared fear and a simmering anger. They were united, not by choice, but by the shared trauma of their experiences, their individual stories woven together by the threads of a chilling truth.

He'd stumbled into this alliance by accident, the whispers of the society's influence echoing through the dark corridors of his investigation. He had found his sister's killer, but in the process, he'd unearthed something far more sinister. A labyrinthine web of power, a clandestine organization operating in the shadows, pulling the strings of influence, manipulating events, and leaving a trail of shattered lives in their wake.

The faces before him, once strangers bound by their individual tragedies, now mirrored a collective defiance. There was Emily, the woman he'd once suspected, her eyes now hardened, her voice laced with a steel he hadn't heard before. There was Michael, his haunted expression replaced by a simmering fury, the years of suppressed guilt fueling his resolve. And there was a handful of others, each bearing the weight of their personal stories, now ready to join the fight for justice.

"We can't hide anymore," John said, his voice resonating with the conviction that had begun to consume him.

"They've been operating in the shadows for too long, pulling the strings, using us like pawns in their twisted game. We are not pawns. We are not victims. We are survivors. And we are stronger together."

A murmur of agreement rippled through the group, a collective sigh of relief that they were not alone. "We are not alone," echoed Emily, her voice carrying the weight of years of unspoken suffering. "We are not alone."

The words felt like a mantra, a promise whispered in the darkness. They had stumbled upon a truth so profound, so terrifying that it had shattered their individual realities. But in the depths of that shared fear, they had found a strength they never knew they possessed. They had discovered the power of unity, a force that could topple empires, that could dismantle the elaborate facade of a society built on lies and manipulation.

The price of truth was high, John knew, but he was no longer alone. He had the weight of his sister's memory, the burning need to find closure, and the unwavering conviction that justice would prevail. But the weight of their collective truth, the shared burden of their individual stories, the collective roar of their combined defiance, would be their greatest weapon. They would face the shadows, and in the blinding light of their unity, they would expose the truth.

The meeting was a turning point, a moment of reckoning that would forever alter the course of their lives. They had agreed to share their stories, to compile the fragments of their individual experiences, to form a unified front, a coalition of courage against a force that had seemed invincible.

They would learn to navigate the labyrinthine corridors of the secret society's influence, exposing their network, unraveling their secrets, and confronting their corrupt system with a force they had never known they possessed. They would face the shadows, and they would not back down.

Their stories were powerful, a tapestry woven with threads of manipulation, deception, and the agonizing realization of their own vulnerability. They were stories that had been silenced, buried beneath layers of fear and doubt.

As they shared their experiences, a sense of shared understanding emerged. Their individual struggles had been mirrored in one another's narratives, a chilling symphony of betrayal, manipulation, and the terrifying realization that they had been manipulated for years.

"I never realized how deep it went," Michael said, his voice trembling with a mixture of fear and anger. "I thought it was just me, that I was somehow the anomaly. But listening to you all, hearing your stories, it's like a piece of the puzzle finally clicked into place."

John nodded, understanding. "I thought it was just my sister, that it was a personal vendetta, a twisted act of revenge. But it's not. It's a system. A machine designed to control, to manipulate, and to silence."

Emily's gaze hardened. "They preyed on our weaknesses, our vulnerabilities. They turned our greatest fears into weapons, twisting our narratives to their own advantage."

The room fell silent as each individual absorbed the gravity of their collective experience. Their stories were a testament to the insidious nature of the society, a chilling reminder of how easily they had been manipulated.

But in the face of that collective truth, a new feeling emerged. A shared sense of resilience, a collective vow to fight back. They had been silenced for too long, but their stories, their truth, would no longer be buried beneath the layers of deceit.

They would expose their tormentors, they would reclaim their narratives, and they would stand together, united by their collective truth. They would become the force that would dismantle the society, exposing its dark secrets and exposing the vulnerability of its elaborate facade.

John's heart throbbed with a newfound determination. The price of truth was high, but it was a price he was willing to pay. He had tasted the bitterness of loss, but he had also glimpsed the promise of a future, a future where their stories, their truth, would be their salvation.

And the battle had just begun.

The weight of the decision pressed down on John, heavy and suffocating. He understood the risks, the price he might have to pay for exposing the truth about the secret society. It wouldn't just be a professional risk, the kind that might cost him his job or reputation. It was a life-or-death gamble, a gamble that could leave him with nothing, everything he held dear, swept away in a tide of retribution.

He knew the society's methods: subtle intimidation, whispers of threats, and the ever-present shadow of violence that hung over their victims. Their grip on the city was insidious, a web of corruption that snaked its way through every level of power, silencing dissent with a quiet efficiency that chilled him to the bone.

But John was not easily deterred. His sister's disappearance, the years of searching, the agonizing lack of answers, had hardened him. He had seen the darkness lurking beneath the surface of the city, the ugliness that hid behind polite smiles and whispered conversations. And he had sworn to himself that no one would ever be allowed to suffer the same fate as Sarah.

He knew the cost of silence, the price paid by those who chose to turn a blind eye. He had seen the fear in the eyes of those who had been silenced, the broken spirits of those who had been forced to accept the truth of their powerlessness. And he refused to be another victim.

John understood that exposing the society would not be easy. He would be facing a network of powerful individuals, each with a stake in the status quo. They wouldn't hesitate to protect their interests, to silence anyone who dared to challenge their authority.

The risk was immense. But so was the potential reward. He could bring justice to his sister, the truth that had eluded him for so long. He could protect others from the society's corrupt influence, prevent them from suffering the same fate as Sarah. He could finally break the chains of silence that had bound the city for so long, exposing the dark secrets that lurked beneath its shimmering surface.

John looked at the file in his hand, the evidence he had gathered over months of painstaking investigation. It was a fragile thing, a fragile thread that could unravel at any moment, leaving him with nothing but the cold certainty of failure. But he refused to be cowed, refused to let fear dictate his actions.

He had stared into the abyss, into the heart of the darkness that had consumed Sarah. He had seen the ugliness of the world, the depravity that hid in plain sight. And he had seen the strength of the human spirit, the indomitable will to fight back against the forces of darkness.

John knew that the price of truth was high. But he was willing to pay it. He was willing to risk everything, to stand against the tide of corruption, to bring justice to his sister and to protect others from the shadows that threatened to engulf the city.

His resolve hardened, his heart filled with a fierce determination. The fight for truth was never easy, but he was prepared to face the storm. The price of truth was high, but it was a price he was willing to pay. He would fight for justice, for Sarah, and for the city he loved.

John knew that his journey would be fraught with danger. He understood that he might not come out of it alive. But he was willing to take the risk. Because the truth, he knew, was worth fighting for, even at the cost of his life.

He had a plan, a strategy that he had meticulously crafted over weeks of meticulous planning. He had identified the society's weaknesses, their vulnerabilities, the cracks in their seemingly impenetrable armor. And he was prepared to exploit those weaknesses, to strike at their heart and bring them down.

His first step was to gather his allies. He knew that he couldn't do this alone. He needed people he could trust, people who shared his commitment to justice, people who were willing to risk everything to bring down the secret society.

His network of contacts, forged over years of working as a detective, had provided him with a handful of leads, individuals who had been targeted by the society and had managed to escape their clutches. He had reached out to them, offering them a chance to fight back, to join forces and strike a blow against the enemy.

One of these individuals was a former journalist, Sarah,

who had been forced to flee the city after uncovering the society's involvement in a series of corrupt business deals. Sarah had been threatened, harassed, and finally forced to silence, but she was still determined to expose the truth.

Another ally was Michael, a former lawyer who had been involved in a high-profile case against the society. He had been intimidated, threatened, and ultimately forced to withdraw from the case, but he was still haunted by what he had seen. He had promised himself that he would do everything in his power to bring the society down.

John knew that these individuals were the best he could hope for, a ragtag group of survivors who had each faced the society's wrath and had lived to tell the tale. They were hardened, experienced, and determined. They were the perfect team to take on the secret society and bring them down.

The plan was ambitious, audacious, and potentially suicidal. But it was the only chance they had. John knew that they were facing a formidable enemy, an enemy with a history of silencing dissent and crushing opposition. But he also knew that they had something the society lacked: truth.

They had the truth about the society's crimes, the evidence of their corruption, and the unwavering commitment to expose their dark secrets. They had the power of truth, and they were prepared to use it to bring down the society and liberate the city.

Their first move was to leak a series of documents to the media, exposing the society's involvement in a series of criminal activities. The documents were carefully selected, a strategic mix of evidence that would damage the society's reputation and expose their influence.

The leaks had an immediate impact. The media was abuzz with the news, the public was outraged, and the government was forced to take notice. The secret society was caught off guard, their carefully cultivated facade of respectability crumbling under the weight of public scrutiny.

John and his allies knew they had to keep the pressure on. Their next move was to contact law enforcement, providing them with the evidence they needed to launch a full-scale investigation into the society's activities.

But the society was fighting back. Their agents were dispatched to silence the leaks, to intimidate the media, and to discredit John and his allies. The pressure was mounting, the danger escalating with each passing day.

But John refused to back down. He knew that he had to keep fighting, to keep exposing the truth, to keep the pressure on the society until they were brought down.

He understood that the stakes were high, that he was playing a dangerous game. He knew that the society would stop at nothing to silence him, to protect their interests. But he was determined to see this through, to bring justice to his sister, to protect others from the society's corrupt influence, and to liberate the city from the shackles of their control.

He had come too far, risked too much, and he was not about to back down now. The price of truth was high, but it was a price he was willing to pay.

The air crackled with anticipation. John, surrounded by his newfound allies, felt the weight of their mission press down on him. Their faces, once filled with doubt and fear, now reflected a hardened resolve. They were no longer just individuals, they were a collective force against a sinister entity – the secret society.

Their journey to expose the society's crimes had been perilous. Each step forward had been met with resistance, their every move carefully monitored. They had learned to navigate the treacherous landscape of deceit, where whispers carried more weight than shouts. They had delved into the society's inner workings, revealing a web of interconnected individuals, each playing a crucial role in maintaining the society's sinister grip.

The revelations had been shocking. They discovered that the society's reach extended far beyond their initial assumptions. It wasn't just a group of individuals with a shared interest in power; it was a meticulously crafted machine of influence, its tendrils entangling the very fabric of society. It had infiltrated government agencies, manipulated financial institutions, and even had its hands in the media, effectively controlling the narrative surrounding its nefarious activities.

John and his allies knew that their task was immense. They were facing a formidable enemy, one that operated in the shadows, protected by a system of corruption and silence. Yet, they pressed on, fueled by a shared sense of purpose and a fierce determination to bring down this corrupt empire.

They gathered evidence piece by piece, meticulously documenting the society's transgressions. Each document they secured, each witness they contacted, felt like a brick in the wall they were building to expose the truth. They understood that their efforts were not just about bringing justice to the victims, but about safeguarding the future, ensuring that the society's power wouldn't corrupt the lives of countless others.

They faced threats and intimidation attempts. John, once a seasoned detective, found himself constantly looking over his shoulder, his every move scrutinized. The secret society's agents, trained in the art of subtle intimidation, made their presence known, leaving chilling reminders of the consequences of their actions.

But John was not alone. He had forged a bond with his allies, a pact forged in the crucible of shared adversity. They had become more than colleagues; they were a family, united by a common purpose. Their collective strength stemmed from their shared grief, their unwavering belief in justice, and their determination to ensure that Sarah's story wouldn't be another forgotten footnote in the annals of unsolved cases.

They realized that their fight wasn't just about exposing the truth, it was about changing the system itself. They were not simply tearing down the society; they were aiming to dismantle the very foundations of corruption that had allowed it to flourish for so long. Their goal was to break the cycle of silence and fear, to create a society where truth and justice were paramount.

They knew they were fighting a war, not just a battle. They knew the fight would be long and arduous, filled with setbacks and uncertainties. But they refused to be deterred. They were fighting for Sarah, for all the victims, for a future where truth could shine through, a future where the shadows of deceit could no longer shroud the truth.

The stakes were high. They understood that their actions could have devastating consequences. They could lose their jobs, their reputations, even their lives. But they were willing to risk it all. They had seen the devastating impact of the society's crimes. They had witnessed the pain and suffering it inflicted on innocent people. They knew they couldn't stand by and let it continue.

John felt a surge of determination course through him. He was no longer just a detective, he was a warrior. He was fighting for justice, for truth, and for a world where the shadows of corruption could no longer hide. And in the darkest moments, when fear threatened to consume him, he would remember Sarah, and the strength he had found in her memory. He would remember their shared bond, and the unwavering hope they held for a brighter future. They were fighting for the truth, and they would not surrender.

244

Chapter 14: The Unmasking of the Truth

The weight of the truth hung heavy in the air, a tangible entity John could almost reach out and touch. The secret society, long hidden in the shadows, was finally being unveiled. The carefully crafted facade of legitimacy had crumbled, revealing a web of deceit, corruption, and manipulation that stretched across the city, reaching its tendrils into every corner of society.

John and his allies, a ragtag group of individuals united by their shared experience with the secret society, had meticulously pieced together the evidence, painstakingly building a case that would expose the organization's nefarious activities. They had worked tirelessly, their efforts fueled by a burning desire for justice and a deep-seated belief in the power of truth.

Their strategy was multi-pronged, a coordinated assault designed to dismantle the society's influence and cripple its ability to operate with impunity. They leaked damning evidence to trusted journalists, stories that would shake the foundations of the city and spark public outrage. The media, hungry for a story with the potential to expose corruption at the highest levels, ran with it, disseminating the information far and wide.

Simultaneously, John and his allies made contact with law enforcement agencies, presenting their evidence and seeking their support. They knew that gaining the trust of the authorities wouldn't be easy. The secret society had infiltrated law enforcement, leaving John and his allies facing an uphill battle. But they pressed on, their resolve unwavering, their faith in the system not entirely extinguished.

The public response was swift and powerful. The revelations about the secret society's crimes ignited public anger, prompting calls for accountability and an end to the organization's reign of terror. Protests erupted across the city, citizens demanding justice and a clean break from the society's corrupting influence.

Inside the secret society, panic began to set in. The carefully constructed walls of their secrecy had crumbled, their carefully woven web of deception unraveling before their very eyes. They scrambled to contain the damage, desperately trying to silence their critics and maintain control.

John and his allies, emboldened by the public's response and the growing support from law enforcement, continued their relentless pursuit. They followed the trail of the secret society, uncovering more layers of their operation, exposing their intricate network of influence, and revealing the names of the individuals who had played a part in their crimes.

The society, once a powerful force operating in the shadows, found themselves under siege, their actions scrutinized, their influence dwindling. Their power, built on fear and intimidation, began to wane as their secrets were laid bare. Arrests were made, prosecutions initiated, and the machinery of justice began to turn against them.

John, standing at the center of the storm he had unleashed, felt a bittersweet sense of satisfaction. His mission, to uncover the truth and bring those responsible to justice, was nearing its conclusion. But he also knew that the fight for truth and justice was an ongoing one, that there would always be those who sought to operate in the shadows, seeking to corrupt and manipulate.

He looked out at the city, a city that had been awakened to the truth, a city that was ready to stand up for what was right. He knew that his fight was far from over, that the scars of the past would remain, but he also knew that he had made a difference, that he had helped to create a world where truth and justice had a chance to prevail.

He glanced at the vintage camera, the very camera that had held the blurry photo, the photograph that had ignited his journey. It sat on his desk, a silent testament to the power of a single image to expose a hidden truth.

He picked it up, feeling the weight of its history in his hands. He thought about Sarah, his sister, and the sacrifices she had made, the truth she had sought to expose. He knew that her memory would live on, her legacy intertwined with his own fight for justice.

The battle for truth had been long and arduous, but the victory, though bittersweet, felt profound. The secret society, once a powerful force, was now a crumbling edifice, their secrets exposed, their influence waning. The city, once shrouded in the shadows of their power, was now bathed in the light of truth and justice.

John, the man who had dared to challenge the shadows, stood tall, his spirit unyielding. He knew that the fight for truth was never truly over, that the world was a complex tapestry woven with light and darkness. But he also knew that there were those who would stand up against the darkness, who would fight for what was right. He knew, deep down, that the future held a glimmer of hope, a promise that the fight for truth and justice would continue, generation after generation.

John's strategy was starting to bear fruit. The Society's network, once shrouded in secrecy, was becoming increasingly visible. Whispers turned into murmurs, and murmurs into outright accusations. The public, previously unaware of the extent of the Society's machinations, were now outraged. The media, sensing a story that could shake the foundations of their nation, dug deeper, unearthing more and more evidence of the Society's crimes. The air crackled with anticipation, a palpable tension hanging over the city.

John, along with his allies – the handful of individuals who had dared to stand against the Society's power – felt a surge of hope. Their tireless efforts, their willingness to risk everything for truth and justice, were starting to have a tangible effect. The Society, once invincible, was now faltering, its grip on the city weakening.

The first domino to fall was the arrest of one of the

Society's most prominent members, a wealthy businessman who had used his influence to further the Society's agenda. The man, a master of disguise, had managed to maintain a seemingly impeccable reputation, but John's meticulous investigation unearthed a trail of corruption that could no longer be ignored. The man's arrest sent shockwaves through the city, a symbol of the Society's vulnerability.

More arrests followed, each one chipping away at the Society's power. The government, facing mounting pressure from the public and the media, finally decided to take action. A special task force was formed, led by a seasoned prosecutor known for her relentless pursuit of justice. She vowed to bring the Society's members to justice, to hold them accountable for their crimes.

The Society's power brokers, sensing their grip slipping, began to panic. They realized that the tide had turned. The public outcry against their corruption, fueled by John's revelations, was relentless. They were no longer able to operate in the shadows, their crimes exposed for all to see. The once-invincible Society was now a target, vulnerable to the justice they had so long evaded.

John's efforts, driven by his unwavering determination to find justice for his sister, had sparked a movement. People across the city were now speaking out against corruption, demanding accountability. They were no longer willing to tolerate a system that allowed the powerful to operate with impunity. The Society's grip on the city, once so tight, was now loosening.

John, watching as the Society crumbled, felt a sense of bittersweet satisfaction. He knew that Sarah would have been proud. Her disappearance had been the catalyst for this change, her story a wake-up call for a society that had grown complacent. He had brought justice to his sister, but the cost had been high. The investigation had taken its toll, leaving scars that would never fully heal.

The city, once a place of fear and uncertainty, was now a place of hope. The Society's fall marked a new beginning, a chance for a more just and equitable future. John, though weary from the fight, knew that the battle was far from over. There were still secrets to be uncovered, truths to be revealed, and justice to be served. He had started a movement, a wave of change that would ripple through the city, leaving a lasting impact on its future. His fight for truth and justice had only just begun.

The air crackled with a palpable energy as John stood before the packed courtroom, his gaze sweeping over the faces of the families he had helped, the journalists eager to capture every detail, and the jury members who held the weight of justice in their hands. The trial had been long and arduous, a grueling battle against a system that had been designed to protect the guilty and silence the truth. But John had persevered, driven by a deep sense of justice and the memory of his sister, Sarah, who had been stolen away by the very forces he was now confronting.

John's investigation had become a beacon of hope, a testament to the indomitable human spirit's ability to fight for what is right, even in the face of insurmountable odds. His dedication to uncovering the truth had inspired others to come forward, sharing their own stories of injustice and suffering at the hands of the secret society. He had exposed their network of corruption, their insidious influence that had permeated every facet of society, and brought down their power from within.

The courtroom was a testament to his success. The families who had been wronged, the individuals who had been silenced for speaking out against the secret society, were all there, their faces etched with a mixture of relief, gratitude, and a newfound sense of hope. The weight of the secret society's crimes had been lifted, their reign of terror finally brought to an end. John could see the flicker of empowerment in their eyes, a recognition that they were no longer victims but survivors, their voices finally heard.

John had been a driving force in this transformation, a relentless investigator who had refused to be deterred by danger or intimidation. He had risked everything – his career, his reputation, even his life – to bring the truth to light. The weight of his actions was evident in the solemnity of the courtroom, the silence broken only by the occasional sniffle or choked sob. Justice, though long delayed, had finally been served.

The jurors filed into the room, their faces solemn, their eyes betraying the gravity of the decision they were about to make. John watched them with a mixture of anticipation and anxiety, the years of pain and struggle culminating in this single moment. The judge read the verdict, his words echoing through the silent courtroom, confirming the guilty verdict on every charge against the members of the secret society. A collective sigh of relief swept through the room, a palpable wave of emotion that rippled through the attendees.

The courtroom erupted in applause as the guilty verdict was read. The families cheered, tears of joy streaming down their faces, embracing each other with a renewed sense of hope. John stood among them, a silent observer, his heart heavy with the burden of the past but also filled with a deep sense of satisfaction. He had brought justice to his sister, Sarah, and to countless others who had been silenced by the secret society.

His investigation had been more than just a pursuit of justice; it had been a journey of self-discovery, a confrontation with his own vulnerabilities and fears. He had been forced to face the darkness within himself, the pain of his sister's loss, and the resilience of the human spirit. He had learned that the fight for justice is an ongoing battle, that there will always be those who seek to exploit and corrupt, but also that there are those who will stand up against them, who will fight for what is right.

John's journey had been long and arduous, but it had also been transformative. He had emerged from the shadows, a stronger and more resilient individual, a champion for truth and justice. He had left a lasting legacy, a testament to the power of perseverance and the importance of fighting for what is right, even in the face of adversity. His actions had inspired others to speak out, to stand up against corruption, and to believe in the possibility of a better tomorrow.

As the courtroom cleared, John stood alone, his gaze fixed on the empty jury box. The weight of the past still clung to him, but he felt a glimmer of hope for the future. He knew that the fight for justice was never truly over, that there would always be those who sought to exploit and corrupt, but he also knew that there were countless individuals who were willing to stand up against them. The world was full of heroes, both big and small, who were fighting for a better tomorrow.

John carried the memory of his sister, Sarah, with him, a constant reminder of the importance of justice and the enduring power of love. The Skeleton's Lens, the vintage camera that had captured a fleeting glimpse of Sarah's final moments, now represented a symbol of the enduring legacy of her life and the fight for truth and justice that it had inspired. John knew that his journey was far from over, that there were still stories to be told, injustices to be righted, and truths to be unveiled. But he carried with him the unwavering belief that the fight for a better tomorrow was worth every struggle, every sacrifice, every risk. For Sarah, for the victims, and for the future of a more just and equitable world, John knew that he would continue to fight, to stand up for truth and justice, to carry the torch of hope forward.

John's journey has been a long and arduous one. He's faced danger, betrayal, and loss. But he's also found strength, resilience, and a renewed sense of purpose. His sister Sarah's disappearance haunted him for decades, and he finally found closure in uncovering the truth, but it came at a cost. The price of freedom was a heavy one, etched in the scars of his past and the constant reminder of the fragility of life.

He had faced off against a secret society, a network of powerful and influential individuals operating in the shadows. They manipulated events, influenced people, and thrived on corruption. The truth about their activities was hidden behind a veil of deceit, a web of lies woven so tightly that it took years of dedicated investigation and relentless pursuit to unravel.

The fight against this organization had been long and grueling. He had faced death threats, experienced betrayal from those he trusted, and witnessed the devastating impact of their crimes on innocent lives. Yet, he pressed on, fueled by the memory of his sister and the determination to bring justice to her and to those who had suffered at the hands of this corrupt organization.

He had learned that the fight for truth and justice was an ongoing battle, a constant struggle against the forces of corruption and evil. It was a battle fought not only in the courtroom but also in the hearts and minds of those who chose to stand up for what was right. He had seen firsthand the power of unity, the strength that came from working together, and the importance of finding common ground in the face of adversity.

John understood that the price of freedom wasn't just about achieving justice, it was about safeguarding the ideals that made a society just and equitable. He understood that the fight against corruption wasn't just about bringing down individuals, it was about dismantling systems that allowed those individuals to thrive.

He knew that there would always be those who sought to exploit and corrupt, who believed in the power of manipulation and deception. But he also knew that there were those who would stand up against them, who would fight for what was right. He believed that the world was full of heroes, both big and small, who were fighting for a better tomorrow.

His journey, a relentless pursuit of the truth, had left a lasting legacy. He had shown the world that even in the face of immense power, truth could prevail. His story was a reminder that the fight for justice was never over, that hope could always blossom even in the darkest of times.

As he looked back on the events of the investigation, he reflected on the lessons he had learned and the changes he had made. The pain and loss he had experienced had left an indelible mark on him, a constant reminder of the fragility of life. But he also celebrated the strength and resilience he had found within himself, the determination that had driven him to persevere.

He carried the memory of his sister and the other victims of the secret society with him, honoring their memory by working to create a world where truth and justice prevailed. Their lives had made a difference, and he was determined to continue their fight.

John's journey had been a journey of discovery, a journey that had led him to confront his own vulnerabilities and to find strength in the face of adversity. It had taught him the importance of perseverance, the value of truth, and the power of human connection. It had shown him that even in the darkest of times, there was always hope for a better tomorrow.

He had come a long way, from a detective consumed by the disappearance of his sister to a warrior who fought for justice and stood up against the forces of corruption. He had learned the price of freedom, the sacrifices that were required to protect the ideals that made a society just and equitable. But he knew that the fight was worth it, that the pursuit of truth and justice was a journey worth taking, even if the path was long and arduous.

The air was thick with the scent of rain-soaked asphalt and the faint hum of distant sirens. John stood at the edge of the bustling city, his gaze fixed on the twinkling lights that stretched out before him like a glittering tapestry. The weight of the past investigation, the unraveling of the secret society, and the bittersweet closure he had finally found with Sarah's case, all weighed heavily on his mind. Yet, in the quiet moments, a sense of peace settled over him.

He had faced darkness, wrestled with demons both real

and imagined, and emerged from the abyss with a newfound strength. The fight had been long and arduous, a battle against the forces of corruption and manipulation that lurked in the shadows. But he had faced them head-on, uncovering their secrets, exposing their crimes, and ultimately, delivering a blow to their insidious network. He knew that their influence would linger, that the whispers of their deceit would echo in the corridors of power for years to come.

But John also knew that the world was a better place, even if just a little, because of the fight for truth and justice. He had proven that even the most tightly woven web of lies and deceit could be unraveled, that even the most powerful organizations could be brought to their knees.

He had learned that the fight for justice is an ongoing battle, a relentless pursuit of truth that often comes at a great cost. He had seen firsthand the human cost of corruption, the devastation it wrought on lives and communities. But he had also witnessed the resilience of the human spirit, the courage that blossoms in the face of adversity.

John had found solace in the knowledge that the world was full of heroes, both big and small, who are fighting for a better tomorrow. They might not be on the front lines, their names might not be etched in history books, but their actions, their unwavering belief in what is right, rippled outwards, creating waves of change that washed away the shadows of corruption.

He thought of the countless individuals he had met during his investigation: the whistleblowers who had risked everything to expose the truth, the journalists who had relentlessly pursued the story, the ordinary citizens who had stood up against injustice. Their stories, their struggles, had filled him with hope, reminding him that the fight for justice is not a solitary endeavor, but a collective effort.

The weight of the past had not disappeared, but it no longer weighed him down. The scars remained, a testament to the battles he had fought, the sacrifices he had made. But those scars also represented strength, a reminder that he had survived, that he had prevailed.

As he stood at the edge of the city, the lights of the future glimmering before him, John knew that the journey was not over. He had a responsibility to continue the fight, to ensure that the victories he had fought so hard for would not be in vain.

He knew that he would face new challenges, that new threats would emerge. But he was no longer afraid. He had found strength in his vulnerability, courage in his fear, and hope in the face of darkness. He had learned that the fight for justice is not about achieving a perfect world, but about striving towards a brighter tomorrow, one step at a time.

He had found his purpose, a guiding light in the darkness, and he would continue to walk towards it, carrying the weight of the past, but also the promise of a future where truth and justice would prevail.

Chapter 18: The Skeleton's Lens: Epilogue

The air in the small, quiet room was thick with the scent of old books and dust. Sunlight streamed through the window, casting long shadows across the cluttered desk. John sat there, the vintage camera resting in his hands, its cold metal a stark contrast to the warmth of his fingers. It was a camera that had held a secret, a secret that had taken him on a journey through the dark underbelly of his city, into the heart of a conspiracy that had reached far beyond his wildest imaginings.

He thought back to the moment he had first seen the blurry photograph, the ghostly image of Sarah, his sister, frozen in time, her youthful smile a painful reminder of what he had lost. He had been consumed by a relentless pursuit of justice, fueled by a fierce love for his sister and a burning desire to find the answers he had been seeking for over two decades.

The investigation had been a grueling test of his strength, a relentless chase through a labyrinth of lies and deceit. He had faced his own demons, confronted the ghosts of his past, and wrestled with the unbearable weight of his sister's unsolved disappearance. The journey had taken him to the darkest corners of his own soul, forcing him to confront his own vulnerabilities and to find strength in the face of unimaginable pain.

He had witnessed the fragility of truth, the ease with which it could be twisted and manipulated, the power of lies to hide the ugliest of secrets. He had learned the dark side of human nature, the depths of cruelty and greed that lurked beneath the surface of seemingly ordinary lives. Yet, amidst the darkness, he had found glimmers of hope, the unwavering support of his loved ones, the courage of those who had dared to stand up for what was right.

He had faced the daunting realization that the past could never truly be forgotten, that its shadows would always linger, casting their long, cold fingers across his life. He had learned to accept the pain, to acknowledge the loss, but also to celebrate the strength he had found within himself, the resilience that had carried him through the darkest of times.

. The skeletal lens of the vintage camera had become a symbol of his journey, a constant reminder of the truth he had uncovered, the darkness he had faced, and the enduring power of hope. He knew that the memories of his sister would always be a part of him, that her spirit would continue to guide him.

His journey had not ended with the unmasking of the secret society, with the exposure of their crimes and the pursuit of justice. It had been a transformation, a peeling back of layers, a journey into the heart of his own being. He had emerged a changed man, his spirit tempered by fire, his vision sharpened by the unforgiving glare of truth.

He knew that the world was a complex and often

treacherous place, filled with secrets and hidden agendas. But he also knew that there was hope, that the human spirit was capable of great courage, that there were those who dared to stand up for what was right, even in the face of overwhelming odds.

The vintage camera, a silent witness to his sister's last moments, now held a different kind of significance. It was a reminder of his own resilience, of the strength he had found within himself, and of the enduring power of love. It was a symbol of hope, a testament to the human spirit's ability to overcome even the most profound of losses.

As he sat in the quiet room, the camera resting in his hand, John knew that his journey was far from over. There were still shadows to uncover, truths to be revealed. But he was no longer the same man who had been consumed by grief and despair. He had emerged from the darkness, stronger, wiser, and more determined than ever to fight for justice and to honor the memory of his sister. His journey had taught him that the past may be a heavy burden, but it could also be a source of strength, a guide on his path toward a brighter future.

John stood at the edge of the cemetery, the wind whispering through the ancient pines and rustling the leaves of the oak trees that guarded the graves. The setting sun cast long shadows across the hallowed ground, painting the tombstones in hues of gold and crimson. It was a fitting backdrop for the memories that flooded his mind, memories both painful and poignant.

He thought of Sarah, his sister, whose laughter had once echoed through their childhood home, whose smile had illuminated his world. He recalled the warmth of her embrace, the comfort of her presence, and the crushing weight of her absence.

He remembered the day she disappeared, the chilling fear that had gripped his heart, and the desperate search that had followed. He had been a young boy then, a mere shadow of the man he was now, yet the memory was as vivid as the day it had happened. Sarah's disappearance had cast a long shadow over his life, a haunting reminder of the fragility of happiness, the ephemeral nature of life.

John had spent years chasing shadows, piecing together fragments of the past, seeking answers that eluded him. The investigation had been a labyrinth of twists and turns, a relentless pursuit of truth that had led him through dark alleys and into the heart of deceit. He had faced the chilling reality of his sister's fate, the horrifying truth of her killer's presence among them.

He had confronted the monsters in his past, the men who had betrayed his family's trust, who had shattered their world. He had unmasked the secrets, the lies, and the twisted motives that had driven them. He had brought justice to his sister's memory, but the pain of her loss remained, a constant ache in his heart.

The weight of the investigation had reshaped him, forged him in the fire of grief and loss. He had emerged from the depths of despair with a renewed sense of purpose, a determination to make a difference, to honor his sister's memory by fighting for truth and justice. He had learned that life is precious, fleeting, and filled with both joy and sorrow. He had learned that love is a powerful force, a bond that transcends time and death.

As he stood at Sarah's grave, John felt a sense of peace wash over him. He had come to terms with the truth, had found a measure of closure. He had learned that forgiveness is not about condoning evil but about releasing oneself from the chains of anger and hatred. He had found forgiveness for his sister's killer, not as a sign of weakness but as a testament to his strength. He had chosen to embrace the love and support of his family, to find solace in their shared grief and to find strength in their united spirit.

The vintage camera with the blurry photograph, a ghostly testament to Sarah's final moments, rested on his desk at home. He looked at it now, its lens reflecting a glimmer of hope, a symbol of the resilience of the human spirit, the enduring power of love. He had learned that even in the darkest of times, hope can prevail.

The world had changed since the day Sarah disappeared. He had changed. The world had become a more complex, more dangerous place, but it was also a world filled with beauty, with love, and with hope. He had seen the depths of human depravity, but he had also witnessed the extraordinary capacity for kindness, compassion, and love. He had seen the world through the lens of grief, through the lens of pain, and through the lens of love.

John continued his work, his dedication to creating a world where truth and justice prevailed. He understood that the fight for justice was never ending, a constant struggle against the forces of corruption and darkness. But he was determined to continue the fight, to honor the memory of his sister, to protect the innocent, and to create a better future for all. He knew that Sarah's life had made a difference, and he was determined to continue her fight.

As the sun dipped below the horizon, casting the cemetery in an ethereal glow, John felt a flicker of hope ignite within him. He knew that Sarah's memory would forever be a part of him, a guiding light in the darkness. He knew that her spirit would live on, an enduring testament to the power of love and the resilience of the human spirit. He would carry her memory with him always, as he continued his fight for truth and justice, a fight he knew would never truly end.

John's journey is not over. The scars of his sister's disappearance run deep, etched into his soul, a constant reminder of the fragility of life and the darkness that can lurk beneath the surface of even the most seemingly ordinary lives. Yet, within the depths of his grief, a resilient spirit flickers, refusing to be extinguished. He carries the weight of his sister's memory, her laughter and her dreams, as a sacred burden, a testament to the enduring power of love and the unyielding desire for justice. He seeks to understand the complexities of life, the motivations that drive individuals, and the forces that shape human destiny. He yearns to find meaning in the chaos, to unravel the tangled threads of fate that have woven themselves into his own story and the stories of those he loves.

His pursuit of truth has become a pilgrimage, a quest to illuminate the hidden corners of the world, to expose the shadows that dwell in the hearts of men. He is drawn to the unraveling of mysteries, the deciphering of clues, and the unveiling of secrets that have been buried for decades. He recognizes that the pursuit of justice is a relentless endeavor, requiring unwavering determination, a keen eye for detail, and a willingness to confront the darkness head-on.

His quest for justice has taken him through the labyrinthine corridors of the past, uncovering long-forgotten secrets, exposing hidden truths, and confronting the ghosts that have haunted his family for generations. He has learned that the past is not a static entity, but a living entity, breathing, pulsating, and evolving with each passing day. The shadows of the past, once seemingly dormant, can rise again, casting their long fingers across the present, threatening to consume the light of the future.

John knows that he cannot simply erase the past. He cannot erase the pain, the loss, the unanswered questions. He cannot erase the memories that haunt him, the faces of those who have been lost, the voices that whisper in the dead of night. But he can choose to learn from the past, to honor the memory of those who have been lost, and to strive for a future where the darkness cannot prevail.

He is driven by a deep-seated belief in the inherent goodness of humanity, the unwavering power of love, and the enduring hope that justice will ultimately prevail. He recognizes that the world is a complex and often cruel place, where darkness can easily overshadow the light. But he also knows that the human spirit is capable of incredible resilience, that the flame of hope can never truly be extinguished.

John's journey is a testament to the power of the human spirit, its ability to heal, to grow, and to overcome adversity. He is a symbol of hope, a beacon of light in a world that often seems shrouded in darkness. His story is a reminder that even in the face of unspeakable tragedy, the human spirit can persevere, finding solace in the pursuit of truth, justice, and the enduring power of love.

The sun, a pale ghost in the early morning sky, cast long shadows across the cemetery. John stood before Sarah's grave, a bouquet of wildflowers clutched in his hand. The weight of the past, the years of searching, the agonizing truth of her killer's presence in their lives, had finally lifted. Justice had been served, but the pain of her loss remained a constant ache in his heart.

He knelt, placing the wildflowers on the headstone. He remembered the day she went missing, the frantic search, the empty promises he made to himself that he'd find her. He remembered the years of chasing shadows, the dead ends, the agonizing uncertainty that had gnawed at him. He had sought closure, a semblance of peace, a way to honor her memory. But the truth had been a tangled web, a labyrinth of deception, a tapestry woven with secrets and lies.

He had found the killer, but in the process, he had discovered a hidden world, a network of corruption and deceit that had stretched beyond his wildest imaginings. The secret society had manipulated lives, orchestrated events, and profited from the shadows they controlled. Their reach had been extensive, their influence pervasive, their hold on power suffocating. Yet, he had exposed their crimes, shattered their illusion of invincibility, and helped bring them to justice. He had stood against the darkness, and in doing so, he had found a sliver of light.

He looked at the headstone, the inscription etched in black marble: "Sarah Snider. Beloved Daughter, Sister, Friend." The inscription was a reminder of her life, her laughter, her warmth, her spirit. He had lost her, but he had also gained something in the process. He had found strength, resilience, and an unshakeable belief in the power of truth. He had learned that justice could be achieved, that the darkness could be challenged, that hope could blossom even in the darkest of times.

The past could never be forgotten, but it could be honored, cherished, and learned from. He had carried the weight of his sister's unsolved disappearance for years, but now, he carried a different burden. He carried the weight of her memory, the memory of her laughter, her kindness, her spirit. He carried the weight of the lessons he had learned, the lessons of courage, resilience, and the enduring power of hope.

John stood, his eyes fixed on the horizon. The sun, now higher in the sky, cast a warm glow across the cemetery. He felt a sense of peace, a sense of closure, a sense that he had done what he could to honor his sister's memory. He knew that the fight for justice was never truly over, that there would always be more shadows to chase, more truths to uncover. But he also knew that he was not alone. He had the strength of his family, the support of his friends, and the unwavering belief in the power of hope to guide him.

He turned and walked away, the cemetery a silent witness to his journey, to his grief, and to his enduring hope. The world was a complex place, a tapestry woven with light and darkness, truth and deception, love and loss. He had found a glimmer of light in the midst of darkness, and he carried that light with him as he moved forward, his heart a monument to his sister's memory, his spirit a beacon of hope.

The years that followed were a tapestry woven with threads of grief, healing, and newfound purpose. John, once a detective consumed by a haunting past, now carried the weight of closure and the memory of his sister with a newfound sense of peace. He had learned that justice, though often elusive, could bring a glimmer of light into the darkest corners of life. The skeletons in his family's closet had been exposed, their secrets laid bare. The weight of the past had been lifted, replaced by a quiet understanding that the fight for truth was a constant journey.

The vintage camera, a silent witness to Sarah's final moments, now rested on his desk, a constant reminder of the journey that had transformed him. It was a reminder of the enduring power of a single image to reveal hidden truths, of the persistence required to unearth the secrets buried deep within the human heart. The blurry photograph, once a symbol of his sister's disappearance, now stood as a testament to the resilience of the human spirit, a reminder that even in the face of unimaginable loss, there was always hope for a better tomorrow.

John's career, once defined by the pursuit of justice, had taken on a new dimension. He had become a voice for the voiceless, a champion for the forgotten. He dedicated himself to working with victims of crime, offering support and guidance, ensuring no one would ever face the agonizing uncertainty that he had endured for so many years. He found purpose in helping others navigate the labyrinthine paths of the justice system, ensuring that no one would ever be left to face their demons alone.

He continued to visit Sarah's grave, a pilgrimage that had become a ritual of remembrance. He would stand there, the wind whispering through the trees, and speak to her, sharing his thoughts and feelings, his triumphs and struggles. The cemetery became a place of solace, a sanctuary where he could connect with his sister's spirit, finding comfort in the enduring bond that transcended the boundaries of life and death.

As he walked through the world, John saw the shadows of the past in every corner, every face, every story. He understood the complexities of human nature, the capacity for both immense love and unspeakable cruelty. He saw the ripple effect of actions, the way choices made in the past could echo through generations, leaving scars that time could not erase.

He discovered that forgiveness was not a weakness but a source of strength, a way to break free from the chains of bitterness and resentment. He had found forgiveness for those who had wronged him and for those who had wronged his sister, not as a condoning of their actions but as a path towards healing and personal growth.

He became a beacon of hope, a reminder that even in the darkest of times, there was always a glimmer of light, a flicker of resilience that could illuminate the path forward. He shared his story, his struggles and his triumphs, with others who had been touched by tragedy, offering them a glimpse of hope, a testament to the indomitable spirit that resided within the human heart.

The world, as he saw it, was a tapestry of interconnected stories, a symphony of lives intertwined, each person playing a role in the grand scheme of existence. He saw beauty in the mundane, significance in the ordinary, and the power of human connection in its infinite variations.

He had learned to cherish the present, to appreciate the moments that made up a life, and to find joy in the simple things. He realized that life was a gift, a precious and fleeting thing, and that it was to be lived to the fullest, each moment a chance to make a difference, to leave a mark on the world.

The Skeleton's Lens had served its purpose, revealing hidden truths and illuminating the darkest corners of the human heart. It had been a journey of pain and loss, but also of resilience and redemption. John had emerged from the shadows, a changed man, carrying the weight of his sister's legacy and the enduring hope for a better future.

Back Matter

Writing a book is a journey, and I am deeply grateful for the support and encouragement I received along the way. Finally, a heartfelt thank you to my readers. Without your curiosity and love for mystery and thriller stories, this book would have no purpose. I hope you enjoy the journey and find yourselves immersed in the world of The Skeleton's Lens.

Glossary

Forensic Artist: A specialist who uses their artistic skills to create visual representations based on physical descriptions, photographs, and other evidence to help identify suspects or victims.

Composite Sketch: A drawing created by a forensic artist, combining features from multiple witnesses' descriptions, to provide a visual representation of a suspect.

Modus Operandi: The specific pattern or methods used by a criminal in committing crimes, which can help investigators identify the perpetrator.

Alibi: A claim that an individual was at a different location during the time of a crime, providing evidence that they could not have committed the act.

Red Herring: A misleading clue or piece of evidence that misdirects the investigation, often used to create suspense and intrigue.

Other Mysteries by Jo Smoak

Paws of Justice, A Murder Mystery

The Case of the Vanishing Heiress

A Hot Air Balloon Chase to Find the Unknown Killer

The Mystery Beneath the Red Barn

The Case of the Pink Flamingo

Murder Every Hour on the Hour

The Pumpkin Spice Poison

The Tragedy at the Christmas Tree Farm

Meet the Author

Jo Smoak is a writer of thriller and mystery novels. She has a passion for storytelling and a love of the unexpected, which is evident in their work. Jo is also an avid traveler and enjoys exploring new places and cultures. This fascination with the world and its hidden corners is often reflected in her writing. When not writing, Jo can be found hiking, cycling, being with her dogs, or exploring the world with her camera in hand.

If you would like more information about Jo, check out her website at www.josmoak.com and https://josmoak.etsy.com. Follow her on social media: Facebook, Instagram, TikTok, and Patreon.